No Way Out

Will Carver has been a member of vicious Tom Ketchum's gang of outlaws from the start. Then he meets Sally Bright. As he falls in love with her, he decides that he has to go straight if they are going to have any kind of future together.

However, Sally becomes implicated in the bad deeds of the Ketchum gang and Carver decides he has to protect her. In doing so, he falls into the hands of the Texas Rangers. Between them and Tom Ketchum, who expects blind loyalty from his gang members, he finds himself trapped in the jaws of hell with no way out.

Only his gun skills can save him now.

By the same author

Top Gun For Hire
Casper's Courage
Trouble at Gila Bend
Kentucky Killer
Two Dead in Three Seconds
Rodeo Killer
Hell Comes to Town

No Way Out

DEREK TAYLOR

A Black Horse Western

ROBERT HALE · LONDON

© Derek Taylor 2003
First published in Great Britain 2003

ISBN 0 7090 7335 6

Robert Hale Limited
Clerkenwell House
Clerkenwell Green
London EC1R 0HT

Typeset by
Derek Doyle & Associates, Liverpool.
Printed and bound in Great Britain by
Antony Rowe Limited, Wiltshire

For Jacqui Mills,
cowgirl supreme

ONE

Tom Ketchum was on a train westbound out of Lozier. Only he wasn't traveling first class, second class or any other class but criminal class. At 1.50 a.m. he and his sidekick, Will Carver, scrambled over the coal tender to take charge of what was Locomotive No 20. Amid the noise of the engine's roar and the song of the train on the tracks, it took a gun poked hard into his ribs before the engineer, George Freeze, realized the train was being held up.

'Do as I tell you and you won't get hurt,' Ketchum, a tall, dark, mean-eyed six-footer, snarled at him, as he pressed the barrel end of his Colt .45 deeper into the engineer's side to emphasize his point.

George Freeze was no hero, despite hating the likes of Tom Ketchum for making train travel less desirable of late. He muttered something but it went unheard amid the locomotive's din. His fireman, though, was a no-nonsense man and his first inclination on realizing what was happening was to raise his shovel and slap it across Will Carver's square jaw. But ever on his guard, Will Carver saw it coming and was quick to snap, 'I wouldn't if I was you.'

When the fireman, whose name was Jim Bochat, didn't seem to heed Carver's warning, Carver decided that since he and Ketchum were there to hold up the train, there wasn't much need of a fireman any more. With one irresistible movement, he grabbed Bochat by the bib of his overalls and threw him off the train. George Freeze saw it and was horrified. He knew Jim Bochat's wife and young family and could only hope against hope that Jim would be all right.

Further down the line another of Ketchum's gang, David Atkins, was lying in wait for the train to appear. He could hear it coming but knew he had to lie low until it was clear who was in charge of it. It soon became apparent that it was Ketchum. For as the train appeared around the bend he could hear the screeching of brakes. It was soon coming to a halt at the prearranged spot where Atkins had lit a small fire as a marker.

'Cut the telegraph wires?' Ketchum asked him, looking down from the fireman's platform.

'Sure have,' Atkins replied, pointing with a turn of his head at a telegraph wire hanging from a pole nearby.

'Good,' was Ketchum's reply. 'Let's blow the safe then.'

Ketchum was taking no chances with the engineer. Before jumping down from the engineer's platform, he turned and struck Freeze a blow on the head with the barrel of his gun that knocked him out. As Freeze fell in a heap to the floor, Will Carver jumped out from the other side of the locomotive. There was a guard's van and one passenger carriage. While he ran down the outside of the passenger carriage, warning the passengers to stay put and not to try anything stupid, Ketchum climbed aboard the guard's van and ordered the nervous-looking guard to open the safe.

'I ain't got a key,' the guard replied in jittery tones.

This was rather what Ketchum had expected him to say.

'Right,' he said, pushing the guard out of the way and making him land spread-eagled on a pile of mail sacks. Atkins was standing by the entrance to the van with a saddle-bag full of dynamite.

'Give it here,' Ketchum said, turning to face him.

Not Ketchum, nor Atkins nor Carver had any experience of explosives, but they reckoned all you had to do was stick a fuse in the end of a stick and light it. Ketchum was the one who made a guess as to how many sticks they'd need to blow the safe.

'You can't do that!' the guard gasped when he saw Ketchum take two sticks of dynamite out of the saddle-bags he took from Atkins.

'Shut up!' Ketchum snarled at him, 'Or I'll tie you to the safe with them. Get him off the train,' he ordered Atkins.

Fixing the two sticks of dynamite to the front of the safe near the door hinges, he took out a match, struck it on his trousers and lit the fuse.

'Get down,' he said to the others, as he jumped from the train and joined them well away from the van's door.

The explosion rocked the train and gave the passengers a fright, telling them exactly what was going on if they hadn't already guessed. But it did no more than rock the train and dent the safe's door.

'Sonofabitch!' Ketchum exclaimed as the smoke cleared and he got a picture of the safe still intact.

This time he attached six sticks of the dynamite to the safe and as well as blowing the door off what was a walk-through safe he blew the roof off the guard's van. The dust and debris had barely begun to settle before he and Atkins were walking into the safe to see what their haul was going to be.

'Well, well, well,' was all Ketchum said, a smirk the size of a broad grin spreading across his face, as he found himself looking at a mountain of cash bags.

Atkins said nothing but just looked on in amazed delight.

'Right,' said Ketchum, 'fetch the horses and let's get this lot loaded.'

Their haul was $42,000, though for years afterwards Wells Fargo maintained it was less than $6,000.

TWO

'Godammit, don't it sink in with none of them that we ain't gonna put up with this sort of thing in Texas!' exclaimed Texas Ranger Captain Bill Foggerty on hearing the news of the train hold-up.

'They hear it,' replied Lozier town sheriff, Jed Broom, 'they just don't take no heed of it.'

'We'll see about that,' Foggerty said. 'Round up the boys and tell them to be ready to ride in half an hour,' he instructed one of his senior rangers.

'Won't they be long gone by now?' Jed Broom suggested to him.

'We've run to earth outlaws much longer gone than this lot, Jed. Have no fear of that.'

Broom knew Captain Foggerty was not telling a lie. He had a fearsome reputation all

13

over the state of Texas for catching his man and it wasn't long before he picked up the trail of Ketchum and his gang. The country was wide open and Ketchum quickly realized they were being followed. He didn't care, though, believing he could outrun any pesky small town posse; either that or lay an ambush and kill them all. This time he decided to just keep on running. Their saddle-bags were stuffed with loot, which had filled him with a wild and recklessly defiant atti-tude to life.

'How far to Tom Green County?' Ketchum asked his younger brother, Sam, who'd joined his gang, despite their father's attempts to persuade him otherwise.

'Forty, maybe fifty miles,' Sam replied.

'Good!' said Ketchum, 'We'll out run 'em, then we'll lose them in the hills.'

'You reckon?' Dave Atkins replied.

'Yeah, and it'll be dark soon. They'll rest but we'll keep going and come morning they won't know which direction we've gone in.'

Atkins wasn't convinced, but Ketchum was the leader, the kind of leader whose decisions you did not question.

'You don't reckon they're Texas Rangers,

then, Tom?' Will Carver asked Tom Ketchum.

'Like I said before,' Ketchum replied. 'It's a posse out of Lozier and nothing to be worried about.'

Ketchum was wrong, of course. He and his gang had robbed post offices and stores and won shoot-outs in bars and had never been bothered by anyone more than the local sheriff and his deputies. But robbing the Harrisburg & San Antonio Railroad had put a different complexion on things. The Texas Rangers had known of their criminal activities but they were way down on their list of priorities; now they were at the top. From petty outlaws, they had graduated to out and out criminals whose activities, no matter how petty or great, were not going to be tolerated anywhere in the state.

'Could be Texas Rangers,' Dave Atkins ventured to suggest, echoing Will Carver.

'Maybe they are, maybe they ain't,' Tom Ketchum said in reply, 'either ways, it don't matter much.'

And without looking at the others he pointed his horse in the direction of Tom Green County and spurred it into a trot. The others followed, none of them very happy at the prospect of being pursued at all, let alone by Texas Rangers.

Captain Foggerty and his men did not make camp for the night, but kept hot on the tail of Ketchum and his gang. There was hardly any moonlight, which made the going slow and treacherous, but they kept on anyway. They drew pretty close to their quarry but in the end were defeated by the hilly terrain Ketchum had counted on.

'Reckon they've shaken us off,' Sidney Barrett, Foggerty's trusted lieutenant remarked as, on bended knee in the growing light of a new day, he tried to bring to life a trail that had gone cold.

'They gotta be in these parts somewhere,' Foggerty replied, making his tired body sit up straight in the saddle, enabling him to spread his gaze far and wide over the hilly terrain that spread out all around them. Try as he might, though, he could identify no sign of human presence anywhere.

'Disappeared into thin air,' Barrett said. 'Reckon they know the lie of the land well enough to have done just that.'

'We'll see,' Foggerty muttered to himself but

loud enough for the others to hear. Then, louder, adding: 'We might as well make camp here for a few hours and catch up on some shut-eye.'

On hearing him say the words, all of his men breathed a sigh of relief. Not only were they dog-tired, they were hungry, too.

THREE

'What are we gonna do with the money?' Sam Ketchum asked his brother. 'It's an awful lot to be carrying around with us.'

'Find some place to stash it. We got friends enough around here,' Ketchum replied.

'Reckon they can be trusted?' Carver asked him.

'Nope, but we can sure as hell frighten them into being so,' Ketchum replied.

They were on the top of a hill and could look down over the valley they had spent a lot of the night traversing.

'Aint no sign of your Texas Rangers now, is there?' he added. 'Told you they was just the sheriff and his posse from out of Lozier. Reckon they went home long ago and are sitting at their tables now enjoying some nice home-cooked breakfast.'

'That's just what I could do with,' Will Carver remarked.

'Me, too,' said Atkins, wishing along with the others not to dwell for long on the subject of whether or not they were pursued by Texas Rangers.

'Well, reckon I know just the place to find some,' Ketchum remarked, indicating with a twist of his head a farmhouse, with smoke coming from its chimney, nestled deep in the valley on the other side of the hill they were on top of.

Not long after, they rode on to the homestead of a wary and frightened widowed lady and her three children, two girls and a boy. It was one of the girls working in a field near the house who first saw the dust of the Ketchum gang's mad dash for the farm. Her daughter's warning meant that by the time Ketchum and his gang arrived the widowed lady was standing on the veranda of their timber-built farmhouse with a loaded and cocked double-barrel shotgun. Her children were in the house behind her, peering through the windows. She was ready for their sakes, if nothing else, to empty the two barrels at the least provocation.

There was, though, going to be no need for it. The Ketchum family was well known to her and the smile that spread across her face showed her relief on seeing that the rider leading the group of men was Tom Ketchum.

'Why, Tom!' she said, uncocking the shotgun and lowering it to the ground. 'You had me worried for a moment. I didn't know who it could be.' In a second the children appeared from inside the house and gathered around their mother's skirts.

'Well, Sal, we was passing by and saw the smoke coming from your chimney and thought maybe . . .'

'There'd be a pot of coffee on the stove,' Sally Bright interrupted him.

'Something like that,' Tom Ketchum smiled.

'Well, come on in. I'm sure there's enough in the pot for you all. And if not, I can always make another. And some food. Y'all look hungry to me.'

The words were music to the Ketchum gang's ears and they all very cheerily dismounted. The Bright's boy, Jim, who was only twelve, had shrunk deep into himself when his father had been gunned down by a rough-neck drifter who had tried to force himself upon the family three years before, and he did not leave his mother's side to go and help the men tie up their horses. Instead he pulled in closer to her, hiding in her skirts as she turned to go into the house.

Tom Ketchum was the first to mount the few steps on to the veranda. 'Hello, Jim,' he sang out to the boy. 'You know me, don't you. Uncle Tom. Remember how your daddy and I used to ride the line for the Bell ranch?'

The boy gave no reply, but simply buried himself deeper into his mother's skirts.

'Jim, don't do that,' his mother sang out. 'I can't tend to Uncle Tom's and his friends' breakfast with you clinging to me like a leech.'

And so saying she shook herself free, while Jim ran off to stand with his sisters, who'd followed their mother into the house and were simply standing by a large farmhouse table. Outside the men were tying their horses to a hitching rail.

'You know this family?' Dave Atkins asked the younger Ketchum, Sam.

'Can't say as I do,' Sam replied, 'but I heard

Tom talk of them a time or two.'

'So what happened to her old man?' Will Carver asked.

When told, he and Atkins were suitably shocked and full of sympathy for the widow and her three children.

'Ain't no one come along to wed her?' Will Carver asked, secretly fancying his chances.

'Don't ask me,' Sam replied impatiently, as if resenting Carver's interest in the widow. 'As I told you, I don't really know the family.'

'Well,' said Atkins, 'let's go in and see if she cooks as well as she looks.'

While the Ketchum gang were tucking into a breakfast of pork, beans and bread, Captain Foggerty and his men, who'd made their rest-stop short, were bringing their horses to rest on top of the hill the gang had only hours before vacated. It didn't take Foggerty long to spot the homestead with the smoke billowing from its chimney. He reached down to his saddle-bags and pulled out a pair of powerful binoculars. Putting them to his eyes, he focused them on the homestead and was cheered by what he saw: a number of horses tied to a hitching rail. It was not a sight one usually expected to see other than outside a saloon in town. Unless that is, the homesteaders had had unexpected company.

'What d'you make of that?' he asked his lieutenant, handing him the binoculars.

Barrett trained the binoculars on the homestead and having refocused them to suit his own eyes, saw immediately what Foggerty had referred to.

'Could be them,' he remarked, continuing to look through the binoculars. 'If it is, they are, judging by the smoke coming from the chimney, inside having themselves a nice old breakfast. I don't see any look-outs posted.'

'Maybe they don't realize we're on their tail,' Foggerty replied, reaching out to reclaim the binoculars and put them back into his saddle-bags. 'Well,' he continued, 'reckon we oughta go down and show them.'

Had he taken another look through his binoculars he'd have seen Atkins and Carver come out of the farmhouse and walk up to their horses to fetch their saddle-bags. The way the saddle-bags bulged he'd have known for the sure they were the train robbers. Had

Atkins and Carver come out half an hour later they might have seen Foggerty and his men descending upon them. As it was, neither group was aware of what the others were about.

Inside the farmhouse Atkins and Carver threw the saddle-bags on to the large farmhouse kitchen table.

'Right,' said Tom Ketchum, 'let's count it.'

They were amazed when they got to $20,000 and there was as much to count again.

'What we gonna do with it all?' Sam Ketchum asked.

'I been thinking about that myself,' his elder brother replied, turning to Sally, who'd been looking on aghast. 'And I was wondering, Sal, if we couldn't stash some of it here for a while. And if you was ever short, why, you could just help yourself to whatever you needed.'

Sally showed that she was only too willing to let Ketchum stash whatever he wanted of their hoard on her homestead, but she wasn't so sure she'd be happy spending any of it.

'I don't want to become an accessory and

have the Texas Rangers crawling all over the place,' she said.

'You don't want to worry about that. Why should they suspect anything?'

'They seem to get to know about everything.'

While talking she began to think of places to hide the money. The children were out of doors playing and she reckoned it was just as well they weren't present to see what was going on.

'Forty two thousand dollars exactly!' Atkins, who along with Will Carver, had been counting the money, suddenly declared.

The rest of the gang whistled in amazement.

'Well,' announced Tom Ketchum, 'we'll divide ten amongst us and the rest we'll leave here. Where you gonna hide it, Sal?'

'I been thinking about that. Hal dug a trap under our bed, which he reckoned no one would ever find or suspect was there. Maybe that's the place to put it,' she replied.

'OK,' said Tom Ketchum. 'Let's get to it.'

They counted out $10,000, which Tom Ketchum set to dividing five ways, two shares to be for him. The rest he gave to Sally, who took it to her bedroom, where, with Sam Ketchum's and Carver's help, she moved the bed and rolled back a number of layers of oiled paper to expose the earth floor of the house. The trap was very cleverly concealed and even with the oiled paper rolled back it was not easy to spot. In a couple of minutes the saddle-bags containing what was left of the hoard from the robbery were safely stashed away. They were just putting the bed back in place when one of the girls came running into the house to tell her mother that a group of men on horseback were riding fast towards the farm.

'What?' was Tom Ketchum's snappy reply, as he rushed to the front door of the house to look out.

He could see the men coming and reckoned they were about a mile away and closing fast. Will Carver rushed to the door at the same time.

'Who d'you think they are?' he asked out loud.

'I don't know and I don't aim to hang around and find out.'

'Get the others and let's get out of here.'

Carver called to Atkins and Sam Ketchum

and in less than a few minutes they were all swinging up on to their mounts.

'Who do you think they are?' Sally Bright called to Tom Ketchum nervously, as she gathered her children about her and stood on the veranda of the farmhouse.

'Your guess is as good as mine,' Ketchum replied, holding his horse tightly reined-in as it struggled to take off in a gallop and follow the others, who were already on their way, riding into a wood behind the farmhouse. 'But don't tell them anything. Say we imposed ourselves upon you, demanding breakfast.'

Sally Bright nodded to show her under-standing of what he said, but she looked frightened.

'Don't worry, Sal, you'll be OK. And we'll be back. Just be brave.'

And with that he was gone, just in time to avoid meeting Foggerty and his men as they charged on to the homestead. Foggerty paused just long enough to ask Sally if she was ok and to gauge by the tone of her reply if she was involved with the gang. Then, satis-fied that she sounded as afraid as she ought to have been if she was an innocent victim, he set off in hot pursuit of Ketchum and his gang, calling out that they'd be back.

Pulling her children even closer to her, Sally Bright sighed, as whom she knew from their dress to be none other than Texas Rangers disappeared from sight.

'Thank God,' she thought, 'the children know nothing about the money!'

FOUR

Tom Ketchum and his gang spread out in the wood and rode like fury, ducking to miss branches, as they waited for lead to start flying around them. They didn't have to wait long as Foggerty and his men began to get them in their sights. Any shot that hit home, though, would be a lucky one. The wood was dense and it was difficult to keep a man in your sights for more than a second or two. One man who, the others later assumed, must have been the victim of a lucky shot was Will Carver. He, though, when he thought no one would see him, circled back to the homestead. If Sally Bright was a widowed lady, he was a single man who wanted to bag himself a wife.

But the others had to take their chances. It wasn't long before the wood began to thin out and soon they found themselves racing across open ground, which meant the fire of the Texas Rangers pursuing them would become more deadly. The Texas Rangers, though, came out of the woods in a bunch, whereas Ketchum and his gang remained fanned out and appeared to Foggerty to be riding off in different directions. This created a dilemma for the leader of the Texas Rangers and left him in a quandary as to which of the gang he should chase after. It was not the habit of Texas Rangers to spread themselves too thinly on the ground and he decided instead to rein his men in.

'Ain't we gonna go after them?' Sidney Barrett, his lieutenant, asked.

'Which of them you talking about?' Foggerty asked him pointedly.

Barrett understood the point his leader was making and made no further comment. The other rangers saw it too, and, inured as they were to riding long and hard, were relieved to think they could rest up for a while and perhaps go back to the farmhouse and grab themselves some decent food and rest.

'There'll be other opportunities,' were Foggerty's last stoical words on the matter.

Sally Bright had barely collected herself and was standing in front of a rather make-do mirror in her bedroom brushing her hair when she heard the voice of her son Jim announcing the arrival of another rider as he burst into the house looking for her. Sally could only feel exasperated, wondering who it was now, as she collected her hair into a bun and pinned it back into place.

'Mum, Mum . . .' young Jim continued as he found his mother coming from her bedroom, calling out that she'd heard him. 'It's one of the men who was here earlier,' he quickly got out.

As she hurried through to the main part of the house, Sally couldn't help but wonder, and dread at the same time, if Tom Ketchum and his men had been chased back from where they'd fled. She thought her fears were confirmed when her eyes fell on Will Carver, who came in through the front door as she drew close to it.

'Sorry, ma'am if I startled you,' Will Carver greeted her, 'it's just that I was worried for you and the children.'

'Where are the others?' Sally asked him.

'A long ways off by now, I should imagine,

33

with those other men on horseback in hot pursuit.'

'You mean Texas Rangers,' Sally informed him.

'I knew it,' Carver quickly remarked. 'I guessed it all along. They been on our tails since we robbed the train.'

'They said they'd be back,' Sally warned him. 'I don't think it's safe for you to be here.'

Carver felt a little bashful and it showed in his face. Sally, a woman of the world, was quick to spot it. He'd taken off his hat and was playing with it awkwardly in both hands.

'I suppose not,' he said. 'But, as I told you, I was concerned for you and the children. I mean, didn't want them thinking you was somehow or other involved in the hold-up.'

'Well, if they come back and find you here, they're gonna think for sure I was. Don't you think you should turn right around and ride away from here as fast as you can.'

It was not at all what Carver was thinking he should do but he was too bashful to come out right away with what his intentions were. Jim saved the day for him by suggesting to his mother that they could hide him. Before Sally could object to his suggestion, Carver declared

34

that he thought it an excellent idea, adding, 'I mean, there should be a man about the place.'

Hardly had the words escaped his mouth, when it became apparent to both him and Sally that the Texas Rangers' return was now, suddenly, happening.

'It's too late to hide you now,' Sally said, suddenly galvanized into some quick thinking by the obvious sound of a group of riders pulling up outside the house. 'You step out with me and we'll pretend you're hired help and that you've just ridden back from town.'

With Carver following behind her, Sally stepped out of the house on to the veranda to greet Captain Foggerty and his men.

'Ma'am,' Foggerty greeted her, tipping his hat.

'You're back soon,' Sally said to him, 'and without any prisoners, I see. Did you kill them all or did they get away?'

Carver, concerned for his sidekicks, was as keen to hear the captain's answer as Sally, only he tried hard to conceal it.

'No, we didn't take no prisoners and nor did we kill anyone,' Foggerty replied. 'We don't always have the advantage and sometimes it's best to wait until we have.'

'That's not the kind of talk people in Texas expect to hear from Texas Rangers, if you don't mind me saying, Captain . . .' Sally remarked.

'. . . Foggerty, ma'am,' Foggerty interrupted her.

'Captain Foggerty,' Sally continued. 'Those men terrorized my children and me.'

'Well, they will pay a price for it, sooner or later, of that I can assure you.'

Having said so, Foggerty switched his attentions to Carver.

'And who might you be, sir, if you don't mind my asking?' he enquired of him.

'I work for Miss Bright and I was on my way back from town when I heard gunshots and raced here to see what it was all about,' Carver informed him, thinking his story would explain why his horse was lathered and why he himself looked a little unscrubbed.

'Is that so?' Captain Foggerty said, not entirely convinced but at the same time at a loss to know what, if he was one of the train-robber gang, he was doing back at the home-stead. 'And what might your name be?'

'Lee, Lee Fox,' Carver replied matter-of-factly.

As he spoke he suddenly remembered the two thousand dollars that was pushed into his shirt pockets. He hoped desperately they didn't show. But before Foggerty could make any more enquiries of him, Sally suddenly made a big issue of her lack of hospitality and insisted Foggerty and his men all dismount and come into the house for coffee and whatever else she thought she'd be able to rustle up for them by way of a meal. Foggerty was glad to accept her hospitality on behalf of himself and his men, who, it has already been said, were feeling more than a little saddle weary, but he was not convinced Carver's explanation of himself was true. The man did not look like hired help. Foggerty felt he had enough experience of low life to know one when he saw one and believed that what he was looking at standing next to Sally fitted the bill of a low-lifer more than he did anything else.

Of course Captain Foggerty was right and meanwhile Will Carver's low-life associates had assumed that he had been killed. Tom Ketchum, while feeling some sadness for his friend's sad fate, cursed that they had shared out the money before being chased off the Bright's homestead. Two thousand dollars had been thrown away and that was a shame.

'Supposing he wasn't dead and has been captured,' Dave Atkins suggested, 'and he's talked about the rest of the money.'

'Na,' replied Ketchum. 'Not Will.'

He and Carver went back a long way and he didn't like to think bad of his old sidekick, but it was a thought.

'Well,' he said after a few minutes' reflection, 'we'll go back. When the dust has settled a bit we'll go back and see what's what.'

FIVE

Whether Will Carver talked or not, Ketchum and his gang found the going rough after robbing the Harrisburg & San Antonio Railroad. It seemed that every lawmaker in Texas was out to catch them. They spent most of their two thousand dollars on lying low. In fact, lying low was not something they found it easy to achieve. They were young men and they wanted to live, which to them meant being in town and living it up in saloons and hotels with good-time girls. When Texas proved not to be as amenable to their wild and reckless ways, they headed for New Mexico. And when their funds become dangerously low Tom Ketchum decided it was time to rob another train.

'I ain't so sure that's such a good idea. You

know you can get hanged for it in this state?' Dave Atkins said to him.

Ketchum looked at him incredulously. 'You worried about getting hung?' he said, almost laughing. Then turning to his brother Sam, he asked of him, 'D'you hear that, Sam?'

'Yeah,' smiled his kid brother. 'But I thought the only way of avoiding getting hung in our profession was to avoid getting caught or taken alive.'

'And that's what I aim to do.'

'I think it's what we're all aiming to do, but there ain't no use being alive if you ain't got no money.'

'Tom, you know we got that money hidden at Sally Bright's place. Why don't we just go and get it?'

'Well, we could but them Texas Rangers are still hot for us. There ain't no one hot for us in New Mexico and for the time being I'd rate our chances as being better here. Besides, I like robbing trains!'

Atkins realized there was nothing to be gained arguing with him.

'OK,' he said, 'which train you aiming to rob?'

They'd been hanging out in Turkey Creek

Canyon, a remote and mountainous wooded spot twelve or so miles north-west of Cimarron.

'What about the westbound flyer at Stein's Pass. It'd be a piece of piss.'

'That's way down in Arizona,' exclaimed Atkins.

'Maybe. But 1 ain't exactly planning to rob the train tomorrow.'

Atkins might have argued more but he realized it was pointless. He'd thrown in his lot with Tom Ketchum and he wasn't minded particularly to alter the fact.

'Well, whatever you say,' he replied.

'Yeah,' Tom Ketchum said in response, adding as he turned to look sardonically at his brother. 'Guess that's about it.'

That was just about it and a few days later they were heading south.

'Where d'you reckon they are now?' Sally Bright was asking Will Carver.

'They could be anywhere's, anywhere's at all.'

Captain Foggerty had taken Will Carver into the Brights' barn and had interrogated him about any connection he might have to the Ketchum gang but Carver had told him nothing and in the end Foggerty had to let him go. Now Will and Sally were discovering an attraction for one another that was quickly turning into love.

'Do you reckon they'll be back soon?'

'They ain't stupid. They'll know Foggerty and his Rangers will be keeping an eye on the place for a while and they won't want to risk the money.'

'There sure is a lot of it, honey.'

'Yeah, well, I don't really want to think about it.'

It was ironic that while Carver and Sally Bright were sitting on a pile and cooing to one another in what was fast becoming their love nest, Ketchum and his gang were broke and in danger of going hungry. They might have done if they hadn't rolled into a town that had a bank. They all saw it at once but only one man had the notion of robbing it. They were at least five thousand feet above sea level and it was early afternoon. The sun was shining brightly and the air was crisp. It was the sort of weather that made you feel good to be alive, only not if you had practically no money in your pockets.

'Think I see a way of restoring our fortunes,

boys,' Tom Ketchum remarked to his gang.

He turned his horse to dismount and tie it to a hitching rail belonging to a saloon opposite the bank. There were a few townspeople about. The arrival of the strangers was noted but that was all. Not much went on in Prescott, least of all bank robbing. As he led his gang up the steps of the saloon, Ketchum cast his eye about him in all directions. The bank was opposite and it looked to him as if it would be easy enough to just walk in and rob it. There was a post office not many yards north down Main Street. Ketchum took note of its existence, thinking fleetingly they could make it a hat trick.

'Beer,' he told the barkeep, as he leaned his bulk against the bar.

The others asked for the same.

'You passing through?' the barkeep enquired of them.

'Reckon so,' was Tom Ketchum's reply. 'Don't seem to be much going on around here to stay for.'

'You're right. Town's growing but this is a quiet time of year.'

The three men took their beers and went and sat at a table far enough from the bar for their conversation not to be overheard. They were the only customers in the saloon. As Tom Ketchum sat back in his chair and raised his glass to his mouth, he said in deliberately quiet tones, 'We're gonna take the bank and maybe the post office.'

Both his brother and Atkins looked at him in surprise. Their surprise was only momentary. They were neither of them averse to robbing anything; it was just they hadn't thought of it.

'When?' Atkins asked.

'Soon as we've finished our beers,' Tom Ketchum replied.

'And the post office?' Sam asked.

'You can be doing that while Dave and I take the bank.'

Sam wriggled in his seat, looking uneasy about tackling it on his own.

Tom Ketchum took note of the fact. 'Only because,' he said, 'there might be more than just a teller in the bank. There'll only be a clerk in the post office.'

'What's the plan?' Atkins asked.

'We'll move the horses to the other side of the street and tie them up outside the bank. Then we'll just walk in.'

It seemed a simple enough plan and with the town practically deserted not particularly risky.

'Sheriff in town?' Tom Ketchum turned suddenly and asked the barkeep.

'Can't say that I know,' the barkeep replied. 'But I ain't seen him today. Nor I have heard of anything happening to take him out of town.'

'Well,' remarked Tom Ketchum, in quieter tones, turning back to the others, 'we'll take our chances. Reckon they're fair to evens.'

He downed his drink and his brother and Atkins followed suit.

'Pay the man,' he said to his brother, who pulled a couple of what were their last dollars out of a pocket and dropped them on the bar.

'Thank 'e, gentlemen, thank 'e,' the barkeep said.

He suspected nothing, having the experience of a barkeeper to know all sorts of strangers are likely to blow into town.

The bank building was no grand affair but that meant nothing. You didn't need a silk purse to hold grand amounts of money, or so Tom Ketchum reckoned. As he finished tying up his horse, he instructed his brother to walk down to the post office and wait to see him and Atkins step into the bank before he stepped into it. Sam strode out and within a few minutes was standing poised to do what he had to do. Seconds later his brother and Atkins burst into the bank with their guns drawn.

'Hand over the money!' Ketchum snapped at the teller, who, the way he suddenly looked up, might have been asleep.

'There ain't much of it,' the teller told him, as he opened a drawer and took out a handful of dollars. 'Wrong time of year.'

'Shut up and just put what there is in a bag,' Ketchum ordered him. 'Dave, go round the back and make sure he's telling the truth.'

With the agility of a seasoned rider, Atkins vaulted the bar and in an instant was snatching the bag from the teller. It felt to him to be painfully light.

'Open all the drawers,' he ordered the teller.

The teller was too shocked and nervous to act quickly without fumbling.

'Come on, come on,' Atkins snapped at him, his indignation mounting as each drawer was opened and shown to be empty.

'What about the safe?' Ketchum snapped.

Before the teller could answer that it was open and empty too, the sound of a gunshot came from the street. Ketchum and Atkins threw glances at one another. 'Sam,' was the thought that entered both their heads.

'All right, get down,' Ketchum ordered the teller. 'Now. On the floor. Now! And stay there or we'll kill yer.'

As the teller lowered himself to disappear behind the counter, Atkins vaulted back over it and he and Ketchum made a quick exit from the bank. They were greeted with the sight of Sam Ketchum running towards them, firing over his shoulder at what was obviously the town sheriff as he went. As he reached them they opened fire to give him cover, at the same time unhitching their mounts and swinging up on to them.

Sleepy though the town was, other men began to appear and take pot shots at them. The soon to be widows of two of them would very soon be wishing they hadn't. So far no lead had rammed home into either of the Ketchums or Atkins. Then Atkins's horse took a hit and letting out a desperate cry it fell to the ground, the thigh bone of its left leg shattered. Cursing, Atkins jumped clear. Tom and

Sam Ketchum had already begun to ride south out of town but they both realized they'd have to go back and get him. There was still plenty of lead flying around but, except for that let go by the outlaws, it was biting dust or slapping into wood.

'Ya!' Tom Ketchum snapped at his horse, as he turned it around and spurred it in the direction of Atkins, who was emptying his Colt.44 in all directions.

In an instant he was swinging up behind Tom Ketchum, who, along with his brother, began to ride hell for leather out of town. The last shot that Tom Ketchum fired hit the sheriff in his left shoulder, sending him flying back into a shop, in the entrance of which he had been taking cover. With the sheriff down there was no one with the inclination to give any kind of chase to the Ketchum gang, who were able therefore to get clean away.

SIX

It wasn't long before Tom Ketchum realized that he and his gang were not being pursued by anyone from Prescott.

'That's what I like about this state,' he commented, as he pulled up his mount and scrutinized carefully the terrain all around them. 'No pesky Texas Rangers to get on your tail.'

'They ain't here,' said Sam, ' 'cause there ain't no need for them to be. There ain't nothing to rob. I got nine dollars forty cents.'

'What happened back there?' Dave Atkins asked him.

'I was holding up the place when the sheriff walked in to send a telegram. Casual as you like until he saw me standing there with my gun drawn. I pushed him out of the way and bolted. You know the rest.'

Atkins laughed but Tom Ketchum scoffed. They all dismounted and counted the money they'd taken from the bank.

'Eighty-five dollars,' Tom Ketchum scoffed even more. 'Pathetic.'

'And we got all that money waiting for us down in Texas,' remarked Atkins.

'Yeah,' Ketchum said in reply. 'Well, we ain't far from Stein and when we've robbed the flyer we'll think of dropping in on Sally Bright.'

'And in the meantime we ain't gonna go hungry,' chipped in Sam.

'I don't risk my neck just to fill my belly!' his elder brother informed him contemptuously, folding the meagre pickings from the bank and stuffing them into a breast pocket of his jacket 'You two can split the nine dollars between you.'

This would not normally be Tom Ketchum's way but he was blackly indignant at what had happened in Prescott and the others knew better than to argue with him.

'There's still a few hours of daylight left. Let's ride,' he suddenly declared, swinging up on to his horse and spurring it into a trot, 'We'll have to skirt Prescott.'

A few days later they arrived at their destination, Tex Canyon, a wild and beautiful wooded landscape close to Stein's Pass, the place they planned to hold up the westbound flyer, No 20. The beauty of the locality was, however, lost on Tom Ketchum, whose temper, frayed by what had happened at Prescott, had not improved any. Stein village was close to Tex Canyon, but they had precious little money with which to enjoy themselves in the village's drinking hole.

'When we gonna take the train?' Dave Atkins asked him.

'We'll rest up here a few days first,' was Ketchum's morose reply.

They'd come across a deserted chinked log house in a clearing in which they planned to hang out.

'Think I'll go into Stein,' Atkins declared. 'I've got a thirst on me. Either of you coming?'

Sam Ketchum looked to his brother for a lead before deciding.

'I told you,' was Tom Ketchum's reply, 'I'm resting up a bit. You can go, Sam, if you want to.'

Sam's thirst, after days on the trail, was as great as Atkins's, but he decided he'd do better to remain at his brother's side. Tom was no loner who could peaceably enjoy his own company and you never knew what he might do if he was left alone with his thoughts for too long, particularly when they were so black.

'Na, I'll stay. There ain't nothing more than a broken-down old saloon down there anyway, from what I've heard. You go, Dave, and bring us back a bottle.'

Atkins agreed to this, holding out a hand for the money with which to buy it. Sam Ketchum had to dig deep for the silver dollar he handed Atkins.

'OK, I'll be back,' Atkins said, taking it and putting it into one of his own pockets.

'Hope so,' Sam replied, watching him wistfully as he rode off.

Stein couldn't rightly be described as a broken-down old town, since it had never really been built up. There was a station, a post office, a store, a saloon and not much more. As he rode into town Atkins eyed the post office, from a natural disposition to see how easily it might be robbed. The fact that there didn't appear to be a sheriff's office gave him his answer. But this was something that could wait until later. In the meantime he wanted a drink.

The salon was indeed a broken-down old shack. It doubled as a general store and bath-house. Atkins, in need of a bath, decided, however, he'd not avail himself of the oppor-tunity and instead went straight to the bar.

'Howdy, son!' Eck Robertson, the store owner, greeted him in surprisingly enthusias-tic tones. He was a big man of Scandinavian extraction who sported a bushy white beard. 'What brings you to Stein?'

'Business,' replied Atkins, downing a shot-glass of redeye, the first poured from the bottle he ordered from Robertson.

'Railway business, that must be,' Eck Robertson ventured to suppose.

'You could say that,' was Atkins's reply.

'Good, good! Well, what about something to eat?'

Atkins responded positively to the store owner's offer and he was soon tucking into a hefty meal. It helped the whiskey go down and he was soon beginning to feel a little drunk. Trouble was, though, drunkenness loosened his tongue.

'So, you are here on railroad business?'

Robertson asked him, as he tucked into a piece of home-made apple pie.

'Me and a few others but they're hanging out at Tex Canyon.'

'Tex Canyon? You mean they ain't coming into town?'

There was another man in the store sitting at a small round table nearby. He couldn't help but overhear the two men's conversation and it made his ears prick up. To him Dave Atkins had the look of a man who'd been a long time floundering in sin. He couldn't see that the railroad company could have any business it needed to do with his like.

'Don't seem as they want to,' Atkins replied to the store owner's question. 'Anyways,' he asked, 'what's the train carrying? I mean, apart from passengers?'

'Well, it depends on what days of the week you're talking about.'

'Any day of the week, it don't really matter. Best days of the week perhaps.'

'Another bottle?' Robertson asked, seeing that Atkins had emptied the first.

Their conversation carried on, with the other man listening ever more intently, until in the end Atkins named a day, the following

54

Thursday, 9 December, 1897. By now he was slurring his words badly. He added that it seemed as good a day as any and both the other man and Robertson swore ever after that they were sure they had heard him add 'to rob a train'.

Meanwhile back in Texas Captain Foggerty was in the sheriff's office in Lozier.

'You mean they've just disappeared into thin air?' Sheriff Broom asked disconsolately.

'Well, not exactly, Jed. Word is they've fled to New Mexico.'

'Well, let's hope they stay there.'

'I couldn't agree more, except there is still the problem of the forty or more thousand dollars they stole from the train. Wells Fargo is creating hell and saying they want it back.'

'They would say that. D'you mean to tell me they are admitting to Ketchum's haul being as much as that?' Broom asked, surprised.

'Not publicly. Privately they are admitting the truth but publicly they're maintaining it was only a few thousand. They don't want every outlaw in Texas figuring it's worthwhile holding up a train carrying Fargo freight.'

'You still reckon Ketchum hid that money

somewhere before going on the run?'

'Yeah, but it could have been anywheres.'

'What about the Bright's place? You still sure it weren't there?'

'We searched the place all over and found nothing but that don't mean it ain't there. I've had the place watched since we chased Ketchum and his gang off and there ain't been any sign of them coming back. Mind you, I ain't convinced either that the hired help Lee Fox is what he says he is. No one around and abouts had ever heard of him, but he works all right and works damned hard on that farm, so we ain't exactly got anything on him. And if he was one of the train robbers, he don't fit any of the descriptions given to us by the engineer, which doesn't exactly give us anything to hold him on.'

'So what are you gonna do about him?' Broom asked.

'Just keep watching him and the Bright's place in general. If the money's there, sooner or later Fox is gonna try and spend some of it. Or Ketchum is gonna come back for it. That or send someone in his place to get it. When either happens we'll be waiting.'

'You could be waiting a long time. Ain't you got other fish to fry?'

'We have, but men like Ketchum don't wait long. They know their days are numbered. He'll be back sooner rather than later and when he does show, we'll be waiting for him.'

And at the Bright's place:

'What you thinking about, honey?'

'Nothing much,' Will Carver replied.

It was evening and they were sitting on the farmhouse veranda enjoying the cool of the night.

'Well, you was deep in thought about something.'

They had been drawing closer and closer over the weeks and while they were still living in a moral way, she was beginning to hope he might be wanting to put things between them on a more formal footing. This was what she was hoping he was thinking about now.

'Truth is, Sal, I was thinking about all that money you're sleeping upon. If we was to spend some of it, we could really make this place into something.'

'And cause a lot of gossip in the neighbourhood, which would bring the Texas Rangers back faster than anything.'

'Yeah, that's the problem.'

'Not to mention, if Tom were to come back for it.'

'Well, my share's in there. I'd only want to spend it and Tom couldn't object to that.'

They both thought for a while and then Sally said, 'I still reckon it's too soon.'

Too soon for that, her thoughts carried on, but not too soon for something else. Carver might have agreed with her, but he wanted any loving that happened between them to be on equal terms. He could love her only too easily but he had to be sure she knew it was for herself and not the homestead that came with her. His share of the money stashed under her bed would at least show her that.

SEVEN

Tom Ketchum had no idea that Atkins had spilled the beans about the robbery. Atkins himself had no recollection of the night he got drunk and so plans for the robbery to take place on 9 December went ahead without concern. Come the day they were simply put into action.

'Right,' said Tom Ketchum when they were all mounted up, 'let's ride.'

What had been a sunny, cloudless day was drawing to a close and it was beginning to feel cold. Ketchum and his gang were dressed in heavy jackets. They were going straight to the railway station on the other side of the village of Stein. The village seemed pretty empty as they rode in.

'What about the post office, Tom?' Atkins

asked, eyeing it as they rode past.

'What about it?' was Ketchum's reply.

'Well, I was just thinking that being as there ain't no sheriff in town . . .'

'I told you already we ain't getting involved in that, sheriff or no sheriff. We're here to rob that train and that's it,' Ketchum informed him firmly. He was still smarting from the mess they'd got into in Prescott and he wasn't risking it happening in Stein.

Atkins, who'd made robbing post offices a career before he took up with Ketchum, looked wistfully as they rode past but he knew that Ketchum was right. Whatever they got from robbing the post office, they were likely to get a hundred times more robbing the train.

They pulled up their horses outside the station and dismounted. Ketchum looked up and down Stein's so called Main Street before striding into the station. All was quiet in town and there didn't appear to be a soul in sight. Inside the station the agent, Charles E. St John, was sitting at the counter.

'Good morning, gentlemen,' he cheerily greeted Ketchum and his gang. 'What can I do for you?'

'You can start,' Tom Ketchum snarled at him, drawing his gun, 'by handing over whatever is in the till.'

St John suddenly looked very frightened. He had a loaded shotgun in readiness under the counter but thought twice about reaching for it. Instead he said, 'Well, there ain't much in it. Never is.'

'Whatever there is, hand it over.'

St John turned to his till and opened the drawer, taking out all of the cash that was in it, which amounted to just over nine dollars, and handed it nervously to Ketchum.

Taking it, Ketchum looked at it in disgust. 'You trying to take the piss?' he said, his voice full of indignation.

'No, mister, honest. I told you there ain't ever much money in this place,' St John replied.

Had not the agent been necessary to his plans for stopping the train, Ketchum would have shot him. First the bank and the post office in Prescott and now this. No self-respecting thief could take such embarrassment for long without lashing out at someone.

'Dave,' he said instead, 'get behind the counter and make sure he's telling the truth.

Sam, you search the place and see if there are any valuables lying around.'

The first thing Atkins saw on pushing his way behind the counter was the shotgun. Grabbing it, he made to strike St John across the face with it but stopped short of doing so. Instead he simply threw it to Tom Ketchum. Then he ransacked the agent's office, rifling through papers and books and throwing them to the ground until he was satisfied there was no more money to be had.

'I told you,' the station agent told him.

'Shut up,' Ketchum said, waving the man's shotgun at him, 'before I blow your head off.'

St John wanted to warn him that it was loaded but thought better of it.

'Nothing,' was all Atkins said as he came back from behind the counter.

'Sam,' Ketchum called out to his younger brother, who'd gone into the freight room, 'you found anything?'

'Nothing worth taking,' came Sam's reply.

'Right,' said Ketchum, looking at St John, 'we're gonna rob the train and if you don't do what we tell you to do we're gonna kill you. Have you got that?'

St John simply shook his head nervously.

Ketchum knew that the train was due within the next thirty minutes and that it would at the moment be labouring its way up the steep grade of Stein's Pass to the station.

'Get your red light,' he ordered the station agent, 'and bring it with you.'

Then they ordered him out of the station to where their horses were. They were going to ride down the line a few miles and lie in wait for the train. When they arrived Sam Ketchum and Atkins set about building a bonfire on either side of the track. They could hear the noise of the steam train getting closer as it came toiling up the pass.

'Right,' said Ketchum firmly to St John. 'Light your lamp and get ready to stop the train. And don't try anything funny or you're a dead man.'

While St John fumbled in his vest pocket for a match, Ketchum told both his gang members to light the bonfires. Then he ordered St John to stand on the tracks in front of the fires and flag the train down when it appeared. While they waited for the train, Ketchum, his brother and Atkins armed themselves with Winchester .44s, which they took from their saddle holsters.

Then they stood far enough away from the bonfires to be out of sight. A few minutes later the train hove into sight and St John began to swing his red light to tell it to stop.

As the sound of the brakes bringing the train to a halt filled the air, Ketchum and his gang ran up to the locomotive. Then when it had stopped Ketchum ordered the engineer and his fireman to jump down from the engine.

'Guard them,' he told his brother, Sam, 'and if they try anything kill them.'

Then he and Atkins walked off in the direction of the express car. They were just a few feet away from it when suddenly its door slid open and a barrage of gunfire was directed at them from inside.

'What the. . . ?' Ketchum exclaimed as he hit the ground and took cover behind a large rock.

Atkins was unlucky. He took a hit in the shoulder and lost his Winchester. It sent him spinning into a small clump of trees, where he lay stunned. Sam heard the gunfire but, being young and inexperienced, did not know what to do. Looking from the two men he was guarding to the direction of the express car and back again, he was gripped by an agony of indecision. Should he run to help his brother and Atkins or should he stay to guard the men?

'We knew you was planning to hold up the train, boy,' the engineer suddenly announced. 'The game's up. Best hand over the gun.'

A look of consternation suddenly spread across the younger Ketchum's face as he tried to decide what to do. His mind was made up for him by the fireman suddenly advancing to take the gun from him. Without hesitating he shot him.

'Goddamnit!' the engineer declared, 'there was no need for that.'

'Shut up!' Sam snarled at him. 'Shut up!'

He knew he had to go to his brother's aid. He couldn't do so and guard the engineer. So he did the only thing he felt was open to him. He shot him and as the man lay dying, clawing at a terrible point-blank stomach wound, he turned to hurry off in the direction of the express car.

He was quick to realize that his brother and Atkins were pinned down by fire coming from inside the express car and that he must avoid the same fate. So, walking as close to the side of the train as to be almost under it, he made his way towards the express car. Although the light from the bonfires either side of the track was not as bright as it had been when the train first stopped, it was still bright enough for Tom Ketchum to catch a glimpse of his brother making his way towards the express car. He could do nothing but laud him and hope he'd get whatever he was going to attempt right. To help him he kept up a storm of fire right into the mouth of the express car.

It wasn't long before Sam reached the up end of the express car. The only means of attack open to him was to fire blindly into it in the hope he was able to hit whoever was in there. From where he was under cover, his brother also concluded that this was his only option. He watched as Sam put down his Winchester .44 and drew his two Colt .45s from his holsters. He watched him as he checked the cylinders and then held his breath as he watched him jump out in front of the express car and empty them into it.

Inside the express car were the messenger and two guards. The railroad had been informed of the words uttered by Atkins the night he got drunk in the saloon in Stein and, while not necessarily taking the slurred words of a drunken low-life seriously, it had planned for the eventuality. The three men lying in wait in the express car were, as intended, completely thrown by Sam Ketchum's actions and momentarily ceased their firing. This gave enough time for Tom Ketchum to galvanize himself into rushing to his brother's side. In the next instance, and before the three men in the express car gained any notion of what was happening, both he and his brother poured another barrage of lead into the heart of it. It soon became apparent to them both that no fire was any longer being returned. They quickly ascertained that this was because all three men inside were dead.

'Where's Dave?' Sam Ketchum asked his brother, as he quickly reloaded the now empty chambers of his Colts.

'He was hit and must be lying over there somewhere.'

Both men began to walk in the direction of where the elder Ketchum reckoned Atkins had fallen.

'What d'you think all that was about?' Sam asked him, throwing his head over his shoulders to indicate the gunfight they'd just had.

'The railroad company knew we was gonna hold up the train. What else?' his brother replied in venomous tones.

They soon found Atkins, who was still alive, if barely conscious. Sam ran to him.

'You all right, Dave?' he asked, hunkering down to help him sit up.

Atkins muttered a few barely audible words in reply but did begin to come round.

While Sam was busily tending to him, Tom Ketchum felt like finishing him off with a bullet from his own gun.

'They knew we was coming, Dave, and only you could have spilled the beans. You was the only one that went into town,' he snapped at Atkins between gritted teeth. 'We could all have been killed.'

Atkins muttered an indignant denial of what he had been accused of, but he was too weak by now to be more rigorous in his own defence.

'What we gonna do now?' Sam asked his brother.

Ketchum was going to reply *what they had come to do, rob the train* but he could see passengers were beginning to disembark from the train and he knew that all they could do now was make an escape. He said as much to his brother, adding, 'Bring him, if you want. Don't if you don't want to.'

With that he went to find his horse.

EIGHT

'You're back?' Sheriff Jed Broom greeted Captain Foggerty as he came into his office in Lozier.

'Not for long,' replied Foggerty. 'We got word on the whereabouts of the Ketchum gang.'

'Is that right? They ain't on their way here, I hope?' Broom asked. He'd gone to a stove, picked up a pot of coffee and with an unspoken gesture asked Foggerty if he wanted a mug of it. Foggerty nodded. He was indeed thirsty after his long ride to Lozier.

'They were in New Mexico robbing trains but word has it they've crossed back into Texas. I've had orders to end the surveillance of the Bright's place and to go and hunt them down.'

'Well, you know I've had doubts about

whether Ketchum hid any of his stash at Sally Bright's. She ain't ever been the kind to consort with low-life and her husband was a God-fearing man,' Broom remarked, handing Foggerty a tin mug of black coffee.

Thanking him, Foggerty said, 'I'm not saying she knows it's there. Or if she does, I'm not saying she's willingly hiding it. It's the hired hand. I'm convinced he was a member of Ketchum's gang who was left behind to guard the railroad's stolen money.'

'Well, you may be right, Captain. But if it started off like that, it's changed into some-thing else now. It obvious to everyone they're very much in love.'

'It happens, even to low-life, I suppose. I'm not happy though about lifting the surveil-lance but orders is orders and we need the manpower that's tied up there, which means, Jed, it's gonna be down to you.'

'Me?' replied a startled Broom.

'Well, you're the law round here. Just keep your eyes open. I'm gonna pay the Bright woman and her so called hired hand Mr Fox one last visit but if I find nothing, it'll be up to you after that.'

Sheriff Broom looked uneasy at the thought

of what might be construed as the harassing of one of the county's families, a widowed one at that. He was aware, though, of how tough and uncompromising the Texas Rangers were and that, while people might not approve of their methods, they appreciated the law and order they were bringing to the state of Texas.

'All right,' he said. 'When you planning to do it?'

It was to be later that day, shortly after noon. Will Carver was doing some repair work to the barn when Foggerty and a dozen or more of his men rode on to the homestead. Startled, he stopped what he was doing and waited to see what was going to happen. It wasn't long before Sally Bright appeared from inside the farmhouse. It was she who by way of a knowing nod of her head greeted Captain Foggerty.

Foggerty knew she had guessed why he was there and it made him all the more convinced she was a willing participant in the money from the train robbery being hidden somewhere on her property.

'Guess you know why we're here,' Foggerty remarked.

'Reckon I do but, as I already told you, you

won't find anything here. You didn't before. Why do you think you will now?' Sally Bright asked him.

'Because we're gonna search more thoroughly. We know the money's here and this time we're gonna find it.'

Hearing what Foggerty said sent shivers down Will Carver's spine. The thought that there must be something he could do ran like a ferret through his mind. He was unarmed, though, except for a hammer, which made his chances against a company of Texas Rangers, he knew, non-existent.

Next Foggerty instructed his men to start an inch-by-inch search of the farmhouse. He ordered his lieutenant, Sidney Barren, to take Will Carver, alias Lee Fox, into the barn. By now Sally Bright's young children had run to her and were clinging to her skirt as she stood resolute on the veranda of the farmhouse. Watching her lover be led into the barn filled her with dread, especially when he looked towards her and she saw a look of fear on his face. She pressed the children's faces into her skirt in the forlorn hope that she could somehow or other shield them from what was happening. Will Carver had proved to be a good father-substitute and had brought a lot of joy into the children's lives, not to mention her own. Sally knew the money would not be worth risking the undoing of that but knew it was too late now to admit to having it. She could only hope her late husband was right in saying that the place it was hidden in would not be found by anyone, no matter how thoroughly they searched.

In the barn Carver was being threatened by Lieutenant Sidney Barrett with the words: 'Now, Fox, if that indeed is your name, we know the money's here, and if you don't tell us where it is, we'll beat it out of you.'

Being what the Texas Rangers suspected he was Carver had already been toughened up by life and he was ready to test Barrett's threat.

'I told you already, I wasn't here when the Ketchum gang arrived and I don't know nothing about any money,' he insisted, standing his ground bravely, but wishing he'd had a gun.

'Yeah,' replied Foggerty, 'we know you've told us that but we don't believe you.' Then turning to Barrett, he added, 'Tie him to that post.'

As Barrett approached Carver he took a few steps backwards, looking around him for something to use as a weapon. He saw a pitchfork stuck in a bale of hay but doubted he'd be able to reach it in time. He was right, for the moment he'd begun to back off, Lieutenant Barrett, a tall, burly man, was upon him, taking hold of him with big hands by the shirt-front and dragging him to the post Foggerty had told him to tie him to. Once he was securely tied by the wrists, Barrett backed off and Foggerty stepped forward to look him right in the face and ask in menacing tones, 'Where's the money?'

Carver began to realize he was in for a lot of pain. He didn't like the idea of it but he couldn't give in, not now, not now that he was in love with Sally Bright, who would surely suffer if the Texas Rangers found what they were looking for. He looked defiantly back into the face of Foggerty and dared him to do his worst. Foggerty simply stood back, turned to face his lieutenant and nodded. Barrett knew what to do. Making fists out of his big hands, he stepped quickly up to Carver and delivered a heavy punch to his stomach. It knocked the wind out of Carver and made him crumble.

Foggerty looked on dispassionately for a second or more and then said, 'The money, Fox, where is the money?'

'Go to hell,' issued from Carver's mouth, as he fought to breathe. He looked more defiant than ever.

Barrett didn't have to wait to be told this time; he knew what to do. He smacked a stinging punch into Carver's face, being careful not to pack it so heavily it knocked him out, however. One of his teeth was knocked out and his mouth filled with blood. The pain of it nearly blinded him.

'Well?' Captain Foggerty asked.

Carver simply spat blood and pieces of tooth in reply. Barrett stepped up to him and grabbed him by the hair and pushed his head back, snarling as he did so.

'The money, we want the money. We can keep this up all day, if you want. Or it can stop now. Tell us where the money is and we'll go away and leave you and your new-found family to live in peace.'

Carver would have spat a reply into his face, but Barrett held his head back so tightly he could barely move his jaw. He didn't believe they'd leave him alone. Had he done so he might have told them what they wanted to hear, but he knew it wouldn't, couldn't, end there. If only, he thought, he'd had a gun on him when they rode on to the spread. So his thoughts were running, when he received another punch in the stomach. This time he fell to his knees. When it became obvious he was not going to answer his questions, Barrett kneed him in the head, practically knocking him out.

It had become more than obvious to Captain Foggerty that they weren't going to get another word out of Carver.

'Come on,' he said to his lieutenant, turning to walk out of the barn, 'let's go and see if they've found anything.'

'Sir,' was all Barrett said in reply.

Despite turning the farmhouse upside down, the Texas Rangers had not found the money. The house looked as if a tornado had blown through it and the children had cried at the violence of it. Sally's bed had been turned over, the Rangers had walked over the trap beneath which was hidden the money they were looking for, but they had not found it. Watching it all happen had filled Sally with anger and dread, but the fear of what

78

might have been happening to Carver at the hands of Foggerty and Barrett was a thought that transcended it all. Finding nothing, the Rangers began to slacken the pace of their search. A sergeant who had stepped out on the veranda saw Foggerty and Barrett walk out of the barn towards the farmhouse. As they approached, he remarked, 'Nothing, sir. Nothing at all.'

Foggerty stood for a moment deep in thought. He was convinced by the way he took the beating that Carver was one of Ketchum's gang. No ordinary farm worker would have shown such defiance. Suddenly he looked up at Sally and said, 'Mrs Bright, this is your last chance. We know the money's here. If you don't tell me where I shall order my men to burn the house down.'

Sally wanted to ask them what they had done to Carver but she knew she had to remain as defiant as he had surely been.

'I told you, Captain, Ketchum left no money here. They had breakfast and then they left when they heard you approaching.'

'Are these your last words, ma'am?' Foggerty asked her, barely able to contain his impatience.

Sally simply nodded in reply. Knowing that doing so was going to bring the wrath of God down upon her, she drew her children in closer and waited for Foggerty's response.

'Burn it,' was all Foggerty said.

Foggerty was not a malevolent man and he hoped the instruction to burn the house would finally make Sally tell him if the money was there. If it didn't, well maybe it wasn't there at all and he'd been wrong in surmising it was. He waited for Sally's response. As he did so the Texas Rangers began to appear on the veranda and gather around her. The sergeant and Lieutenant Barrett knew to pause for a moment before obeying their captain's order.

Foggerty waited. And waited. Sally Bright was either a very strong woman or she was telling the truth. Law enforcers they might be, but the Texas Rangers were not marauding brutes and he decided he had to give her the benefit of the doubt.

'All right,' he suddenly declared, 'we'll leave you your house, but we're taking your hired hand with us.'

Sally would rather they had burnt the house down than that but she knew she was powerless to stop the Texas Rangers from doing whatever they wanted to. As they dragged Carver from the barn and threw him on to a horse, she thought she'd die. She thought she should run and fetch a shotgun. Except she knew she mustn't. If only for the children's sake, she knew she mustn't.

NINE

Tom Ketchum was washing his face at a tin basin in the open air at the cabin in Tex Canyon they had returned to after the failed attempt to rob the train. The sun was up but it was cold, not that the cold ever bothered him. He seemed not to feel it. His anger over the murderous trouble that he considered to be Atkins's loose tongue had got them into still rankled with him. Their money was low again and they were going to have to vacate the cabin that day or the next or risk a posse. It wasn't going to be long, he was sure, before New Mexico law enforcers set upon them. He finished his ablutions and dried his face on a well-worn piece of linen that served as a towel. He'd shaved and groomed his thick moustache into shape and now felt ready for breakfast, which his brother Sam was inside cooking.

'Today's the day we clear out of here, I reckon,' he told his brother as he stepped back into the cabin.

Sam's attitude was to go along with whatever his brother said. Atkins, however, who was still lying on his bedroll with a shoulder that still had some healing to do, wasn't quite so pliable. It'd take another three days of rest, he reckoned, before he was he ready to ride. His wound was still very raw and he'd only just stopped feeling feverish.

'I don't think so,' he commented, 'at least not where I'm concerned. I need a few more days.'

This was the chance Ketchum had been waiting for.

'You can have 'em,' he replied. 'Take as many as you like, but we're leaving.'

'Ah, Tom, there ain't no need to take that attitude,' Atkins said in conciliatory tones.

'Why not, Dave?' Ketchum asked him tersely. 'We could all have been killed back in Stein Pass. It was only thanks to Sam here that we weren't.'

'I told you before, Tom, I don't remember

saying nothing to anyone in Stein,' Atkins protested. 'There weren't no one there to talk to exceptin' the store owner and some stranger.'

'Well, they was expectin' us, Dave, and no one else here went into town, which leaves only you.'

'That don't mean nothing. Railroad company's getting more prepared all the time now. Train robbing ain't as easy as it used to be.'

'Shut up, Dave.' Ketchum suddenly snarled at him, going and standing over him. 'Just shut up before I do something we're all gonna regret.'

Atkins could see he had that murderous look in his eye but still he was not the kind to be so easily intimidated.

'Well, if you're planning to ride today—' he began.

'I am,' Ketchum interrupted him, his tone of voice emphatic.

He looked into Atkins's face, daring him to say another word.

'Aw, come on,' Sam suddenly declared, easing the tension that he knew was rising to breaking point. 'Let's eat this breakfast, before it goes cold.'

There was a long pause while both Ketchum and Atkins continued their war of wills, neither concerned with their bellies but only the determination of each to assert the validity of his position over the other.

'I said,' Sam repeated impatiently, suddenly fearing that if something wasn't done to calm the situation the death of one of them was going to follow, 'this breakfast which I just took the trouble to cook is going cold.'

'We ride, today,' Tom Ketchum reiterated, turning away from Atkins with a look that told him he was not going to be contradicted further.

'OK,' Atkins at last agreed, throwing back his bedroll and struggling to get to his feet. He'd slept in his clothes. 'But I'll probably bleed to death.'

That, Ketchum thought to himself, will probably be no bad thing.

They were going back to Texas and Sally Bright's to get their money. This was when word got back to Captain Foggerty that they had crossed the border back into his jurisdiction and he had been ordered to hunt them down. Back in Lozier, Foggerty had taken Will

Carver to Sheriff Jed Broom and told him to keep him locked up.

'How long for?' Broom asked.

' 'Til I get back.'

'And how long's that gonna be?'

'I don't know,' Foggerty replied impatiently.

'What am I gonna hold him on?' Jed Broom, being the small town sheriff that he was, innocently asked.

'On suspicion of being a member of the Ketchum gang.'

'Ain't he admitted to anything, then?' Broom asked, looking at the state Carver was in and reckoning they must have beaten something out of him.

'No, he hasn't, but that don't mean to say he ain't one of them.'

Sheriff Broom couldn't help but wonder if Foggerty hadn't got the wrong man but he wasn't about to get into a legal argument with a captain of the Texas Rangers. Instead, he said, 'Well, I can hold him. I ain't got no problem with that. But if Sally Bright goes off and hires him a lawyer, the law might have a problem with it.'

'Well,' Foggerty declared, 'we'll worry about that if it happens. I'll get a wire sent down from Austin. If I ain't back soon, we'll get a trial date set. But you don't release him, whatever happens, without instructions from Austin.'

Sheriff Jed Broom knew that the ways of the Texas Rangers were above the law and that the state on the whole turned a blind eye to them. If Lee Fox, the name by which he knew Will Carver, did indeed prove to be a member of Ketchum's gang, he knew the law was not going to be of much use to him. Besides, where would Sally Bright get the money from to hire a lawyer, unless, of course, there *was* a stash of it hidden somewhere on her farm? He agreed to keep Carver under lock and key and sent one of his deputies to nearby Langtry to fetch a doctor.

Ketchum and his gang robbed their way across Texas as they headed for Sally Bright's homestead. In July they robbed the west-bound Texas Pacific No 3 at Mustang Creek near Stanton. Captain Foggerty and his Texas Rangers were about one hundred and eighty miles north in Comstock, where another train had been held up by, it was rumoured, Ketchum and his gang.

Foggerty soon heard of the Mustang Creek robbery and decided to go and investigate. It was said that Ketchum and his gang were hanging out in the Lower Pecos region. In fact they were in Rough Canyon, as Sheriff Edward J. Farr was soon to report to Foggerty. They had swaggered into his town and in rather too conspicuous a fashion had spent extravagantly in the saloon and then in the general store stocking up on supplies. Tom Ketchum's face had looked familiar to him and then he found it on a wanted poster amongst a collection in his office.

He would have challenged Ketchum but he was no hero and, besides, he knew Foggerty was in the area. So, instead, he ordered one of his deputies, James Morgan, to follow Ketchum and his gang, who only stayed in town a few nights, and to report back to him where they were holed up. It was obvious they were going to hole up somewhere nearby because of the large amount of supplies they had bought. Then he sent out another deputy to find the Texas Rangers. Two days later the deputy rode back into town with Foggerty and his men.

'You sure it was him?' Foggerty asked

Sheriff Farr, pointing to a face on a Wanted poster of his own, as he sat drinking coffee in the sheriff's office.

'Sure as cockleburs on a coyote. It was him all right. And there were two other men with him. They had plenty of money and were flashing it everywhere,' Farr replied confidently.

Then he told him exactly where they were holed up, saying that he and his deputies would be only too pleased to take him to the place. Foggerty availed himself of the offer and early the next morning they rode out to Rough Canyon. As they approached the spot where the Ketchum gang had made camp, they saw smoke rising from their camp-fire. It was obvious no extra mouths were expected for breakfast.

They had made camp by a pool in the lower reaches of the canyon. As Foggerty and his men approached they caught site of Atkins below them, unarmed and washing his face in the pool. A little away to his right Sam Ketchum was cooking something over the camp-fire. Tom Ketchum was nowhere to be seen, at least not from where Foggerty and his men had placed themselves.

Foggerty began to form a plan to encircle the gang and was about to inform his lieutenant of the fact when a shot rang out and Atkins dropped to the ground. It had been fired by Sheriff Edward J. Farr, who was concerned to show the Texas Rangers that, if he hadn't acted the hero and arrested the Ketchum gang when they where in town, he was no coward either, now that he had them in his sights.

'Hold your fire!' Foggerty snarled at him, but it was too late, the action had started.

As Atkins lay where he'd fallen, with a flesh wound in his back, Sam Ketchum had thrown his frying-pan aside, grabbed a rifle and taken cover behind a small tree. Not knowing who it was who was firing at them, but assuming it was the sheriff from the town they'd just been in, he called him to come down. Then he opened fire.

'Don't return fire until I tell you to,' Captain Foggery told his men, though more specifically Sheriff Farr. His own men knew better than to act without orders.

Sam Ketchum had guessed accurately where the shot that hit Atkins had come from and he kept Foggerty and his men at bay with sustained fire from his rifle. Meanwhile his brother, who had been attending to more personal toiletry needs than Atkins, and who consequently was some further, if little, distance away from the camp, had been deciding on what exactly he should do. He never went anywhere without a weapon and was armed with a Winchester .44. He would, he decided, have to blast his way to the horses and make an escape. The only problem was, the money from the train robbery was in the saddle-bags and they, along with the saddles, were on the ground by the camp-fire, where they'd been used as pillows the night before. He could ride bareback, he reckoned, to any town but not without money to buy replacement saddles.

He had no choice, he decided, but to get to the camp-fire and grab his saddle. Taking cover behind boulders as he went, he began to make his way to the camp-fire. He was almost there, about to open fire alongside his brother, when Foggerty ordered his men to open fire. He had seen Tom Ketchum making his way to the camp-fire. Sam was hit in the arm, which was broken by the force of the bullet that hit him. As he fell, his brother opened fire.

Bullets were kicking up dust around where Sam lay and Tom realized he had to pull him safely behind cover. But he didn't see how he could without dangerously exposing himself.

'Come on, Sam,' he called to his brother over the sound of gunfire. 'You gotta get behind cover.'

Sam knew this but was almost paralysed with fear as he began to cough on the dust that was being kicked up all around him. Then he took a ricocheting bullet hit in the head and fell to the ground dead.

'Sam!' Tom screamed out loud, stopping firing for a moment and then dropping to a sitting position against the boulder he'd taken cover behind. Where was Atkins? he asked himself.

Looking around, he saw him lying near the edge of the pool. He at first assumed he was dead but then saw a leg move. Then he saw that his rifle was nearby. It soon became apparent to him that Atkins had decided to try and reach it. Despite still being angry with him for spilling the beans about the intended Stein Pass train robbery, he decided to help him out by letting rip with his rifle. Then he thought, No, let them concentrate on

Atkins. It would give him a chance to grab his saddle and saddle-bags and get to the horses, which were tethered out of sight of their attackers.

Atkins only got as far as laying a hand on his rifle before he was riddled with enough bullets to make him sink like a stone had he fallen into the pool as he was shot. But it did give Ketchum, who moved with lightning speed, time to do what he intended. Minutes later his horse was saddled and he was riding north up Rough Canyon, soon to break into a gallop as he hit clear ground. He was well out of sight of Foggerty and his men and it was some minutes before they realized he'd escaped.

TEN

Sally Bright thought she'd go mad worrying about Will Carver. There were people in town who would as soon drag him from his cell and lynch him as wait for the law to decide his fate. She had money enough to hire a good lawyer but it seemed the courts were deaf to his pleas and Carver remained in gaol. Word was that it was the place the Texas Rangers wanted him to be until such time as Tom Ketchum was either killed or taken prisoner. That neither had yet happened Sally was soon to find out. She was stepping out of the house to fetch some water in a pail when Ketchum suddenly appeared, riding on to the homestead.

Tom! she gasped to herself, filling up with a sense of great relief.

Minutes later she was pouring him a cup of coffee and he was telling her how he and the others had assumed that Will had been shot and killed by Texas Rangers the last time they'd had to make a run for it.

'No, Tom,' Sally informed him. 'He came back. He told me he was worried about me and the children.'

Ketchum looked at her for a few minutes without saying a word. There was a look of accusation on his face that told Sally Bright exactly what he was thinking.

'The money's safe, Tom. You don't have to worry about that. It's all still there. Every cent of it. They beat the hell out of Will trying to get him to tell them where it was but he never said a word.'

'So, if Will didn't come back for the money, Sal, what the hell did he come back for?' Ketchum asked.

Sally suddenly looked coy and avoided his gaze.

'Oh, I see,' Ketchum remarked, adding, 'Will always was one for the girls and it was usually love at first sight. You ain't the first, Sal, and you won't be the last.'

She was hurt by the remark he made and

Ketchum could see it but he wasn't the tender sort and didn't feel bad about it. Besides which, he was thinking of his brother Sam and Dave Atkins and of the fact that they were now both dead.

'Sam's dead and so's Dave,' he said out loud. 'At least Will ain't yet, which is something, I suppose.'

Sally could guess how Sam Ketchum and Dave Atkins came to be dead but she asked for the details nevertheless. She couldn't help but be glad that Will had not been with them but she knew she had to hide this fact from Ketchum. He was a gang leader and didn't like his men defecting. She asked him how he had managed to escape.

'I lost the Rangers in the canyons. I was just one man and could hide easily. I could see them coming from whatever direction, no matter how cleverly they thought they was creeping up on me. I left 'em squirreling about in vain and headed for here.'

'And no one followed you?' Sally asked him.

'No,' replied Ketchum in dismissive tones. 'I told you, I left 'em behind in the canyons.'

'So what are you going to do now?'

He thought for a moment. He was no good

without a gang. While Carver was still alive he still had one, or least the remains of one to build up on.

'Spring Will, I suppose,' was his reply.

Sally looked surprised and delighted at the same time. She hadn't thought of such a thing. But her delight at the thought of Will being free suddenly gave way to a feeling of real concern. Will being free would not mean they were going to be reunited. It could only mean the opposite. He'd have to be on the run.

'You sure he'd want to be freed in that way?' she found herself asking Ketchum, without really meaning to.

'Why wouldn't he?' he replied. 'The law's gonna get him one way or the other. They'll either hang him or throw him in the penitentiary. He ain't gonna want either. What man would?'

My man wouldn't want to be forever on the run either, Sally thought but knew it would be pointless to say so out loud. He didn't know the Will she knew and if he did he wouldn't have liked it. Domestic life held no attractions for the likes of Ketchum and he'd assume the same would apply to Will.

'I expect you're right,' she said instead, hiding her feelings from a man whose heart could only be dead to them.

'I'll break him out tomorrow,' Ketchum suddenly declared. 'In the meantime, how about something to eat?'

Sally barely slept all night. She wanted to go to town and warn Will about what Ketchum had planned for him but she knew she couldn't leave the homestead, not without giving Ketchum a good reason and there was nothing plausible she could think of. In an agony of despair she got up in the morning and as she cooked Ketchum breakfast she had to answer his questions as to how well she thought Will was guarded in the cell in the sheriff's office in Lozier. She knew there was usually only one deputy on guard at a time, as no one really expected anyone to come and rescue him. Most people in town, the sheriff included, didn't suspect Carver in the way Captain Foggerty had, and duties about the sheriff's office had become pretty relaxed. Sally, though, hesitated to tell Ketchum this, wanting instead to paint the kind of picture that might put him off trying to spring her lover. Somehow, though, she felt that even if she were to pretend Carver was guarded by an army of Texas Rangers he would not be deterred.

In the end she told him the truth, adding, 'It seems a shame, though, to go getting Will the kind of reputation the Texas Rangers wanted him to have.'

For all the attention Ketchum paid to her she might just as well not have said it. Scoffing down his breakfast with hardly the most desirable of manners, he simply said to her, 'I'll get going, then. You're gonna have to sit on the money for a little while longer. But then we'll be back.'

'What are you planning to do once you've freed Will?'

'Why,' he laughed in reply, 'rob a train, Sal. That's what we do.'

And with that he left the farmhouse and went to the barn to saddle up his horse. Sally would have followed him, perhaps to ask him when he thought he and Carver would be back for the money, but she had the children to think of. They'd heard Ketchum say that robbing trains was what he and Carver did and it was something she wanted to put quickly out of their minds.

ELEVEN

Lozier wasn't a big railroad town. In fact it was simply a watering-hole for trains passing through, but it was growing and getting busy. So that when Ketchum rode into it no one paid him much notice. He quickly spotted the sheriff's office and concluded that breaking Carver out of it should not present any great obstacles. There were even horses tied up outside it, one of which could easily provide a mount for Carver. But before doing anything he decided to find a saloon and go in for a drink. It wasn't that he needed a drink to calm jangled nerves; it was simply that he never rushed into anything without pausing to take a breath.

While he was in the saloon downing a shot or two of redeye, Sheriff Broom in his office was being relieved by a deputy so that he could go home and have lunch. This was a routine they'd gone through day after day since Will Carver had been locked up and was something that was done very matter-of-factly.

'I should be back shortly after two,' Sheriff Broom said to his deputy, whose name was Board, taking his gun and holster from a desk drawer and strapping them on.

'Sure thing, Jed,' Board said. 'Just take your time. There ain't no hurry. And give my regards to Shirley.'

'I sure will,' Broom replied. He took his Stetson from a hatstand and put it on, then stepped out of his office into the broad noon-day sunshine. Looking up and down Main Street the town looked to him to be about as peaceful as it generally was at that time of the day. His house was right at the end of Main Street, about a quarter of a mile distant. He normally walked to and from home, liking the way it gave him a chance to see and be seen by the citizens of the town. Now, as he walked home, he doffed his hat to various people he knew and all was very civilized.

By about the time he got home Ketchum was downing his last shot of redeye and was getting ready to leave the saloon to unhitch his horse and walk it the few yards' distance it was from the sheriff's office. He tied it up next to a strawberry roan that he thought would do nicely for Carver.

Then he stepped into the sheriff's office. Although Ketchum was a tall, dark, not altogether respectable-looking sort of person, Deputy Board did not expect the reply he got to his polite enquiry of what he could do for the stranger who crossed the threshold. Once the door was shut firmly behind him, Ketchum had pulled his gun and pointed it at the deputy, ordering him to try nothing and to get the keys and open Carver's cell. It was difficult to know who was more surprised by the sudden turn of events, Carver or Deputy Board.

'I said,' Ketchum restated to the deputy, who'd become frozen with shock, 'get the keys and open the cell door. And don't try anything funny or I'll fill you full of lead.'

Deputy Board suddenly sprang into action and took a bunch of keys from a hook in the wall behind Sheriff Broom's desk.

'You all right, Will?' Ketchum asked.

'Will?' Deputy Board questioned, as he fumbled with the sheriff's keys to find the right one to open the cell door. 'His name ain't Will,' he said turning to Ketchum.

'It ain't none of your business what his name is,' Ketchum snarled at him. 'Just get that door open.'

Carver, who had been eating a plate of food the deputy had brought in for him, stood up and put the plate down on his bed.

'Tom,' he asked his gang boss, 'where'd you come from?'

'Where d'you think?' was Ketchum's reply.

Suddenly the deputy knew with whom he was dealing. At last he found the right key and got it into the lock of the cell door. In a second he'd opened the cell door and Will Carver was stepping out of it.

'You ain't Lee Fox at all, are you?' Board said to him.

'Shut up and get inside the cell,' Ketchum snarled at him. 'Will, get his gun.'

Carver did as he was told. Grabbing the gun from the deputy, whom he'd come to respect and be fond of over the weeks of his incarceration, his mind suddenly became full of turmoil. That he was a train-robber, he knew. It and thieving had been the only profession he'd ever had. But lately he'd become something else besides. And he preferred it. If he went with Ketchum now there'd never be any going back to it, meaning, no going back to a settled life with Sally Bright and her children.

But what was the alternative? To turn on Ketchum using Deputy Board's gun? It was unthinkable. And besides, he knew Ketchum was quicker and faster than he and that he'd fight back and kill him with the kind of ruthlessness he reserved for anyone who got in the way of his practising his chosen profession. No, he had to go with Ketchum. If he wanted to live to see Sally again, he had to. He had no choice. He just hoped Deputy Board wouldn't do anything stupid. He didn't want to see him come to any harm.

'You're one of his gang, ain't you?' Deputy Board said to him, as Will slammed the door of the cell shut on him and turned the key.

'What's all this?' Ketchum snarled, pointing his gun threateningly in the deputy's direction. 'Just shut up before I do it myself with this.'

Carver wanted to say something in explanation to Board but knew the longer he and Ketchum remained in the sheriff's office, the more chance there was of harm being done to the deputy. So he said nothing to him in reply, instead taking the keys out of the lock of the cell door and throwing them across the room.

'Come on,' he said to Ketchum, 'let's just get out of here.'

But Ketchum was reluctant to leave things as they were. He didn't like the deputy's attitude, thinking it somehow or other rude or nosy.

'What's it got to do with you who he is?' he snarled at the deputy, walking right up to the cell door and pushing his gun through the bars.

Board felt too intimidated to make any kind of reply, something which served to annoy Ketchum all the more. He was about to demand a reply to his question, when Carver said again that they should get out of there.

'Before the sheriff gets back from lunch,' he added, opening the door and making to leave.

Ketchum, though, wasn't ready to leave. He felt there was still unfinished business. In the next instant a shot rang out and the deputy was flung against a wall of the cell, down which he slid, blood beginning to ooze from a wound in his left breast.

'Goddamnit!' Carver exclaimed. 'There weren't no need for that, Tom.'

'He knew who we were,' Ketchum said in reply, pushing past Carver to go out of the sheriff's office and step on to the boardwalk.

Carver wanted to go to the deputy but he knew he couldn't. In the next instant he was swinging up onto the strawberry roan Ketchum had picked out for him and was galloping after him out of town. They were gone before anyone realized what had happened.

As they rode out of town and kept on going at full gallop, Carver had assumed they were going to meet up with the others. It wasn't until they'd put some miles between themselves and Lozier that Ketchum eventually reined in his horse and Will learnt what to him was the awful truth.

'Dead? Both of them?' he queried.

'Yep,' was Ketchum's sardonic reply, as if to accuse him of in some way or another running out on them.

Carver's only thought, however, was that if he'd been with them he'd probably have been dead too.

'How'd you know I was locked up in Lozier?' he asked.

'I went to collect the money we left buried at Sally Bright's place and she told me,' Ketchum replied, staring into Carver's face to see what kind of reaction he'd get. 'We thought you was dead, shot by them Texas Rangers that chased us off of her place. But Sally says you was concerned about her and the children and went back to make sure she was all right.'

'I ain't touched the money,' Carver immediately informed him.

'Nah, I gather not. But what about Sal?'

'What about her?' Carver asked indignantly. 'She weren't your gal, Tom, were she?'

Ketchum just laughed. A dirty, mocking laugh. Carver found himself laughing, too. Not really knowing why but just being dragged into Ketchum's making out that what he and Sally had between them was nothing more than something based on a piece of dirty opportunism. He saw his life of domestic bliss slipping away from him but felt powerless to do anything about it.

'Did you pick up the money then?' he asked Ketchum, once the laugher had ceased.

'No, it's still there.'

'We gonna go back and get it?'

'Guess so,' Ketchum replied, beginning to grin insinuatingly again. 'Unless you'd rather go rob a train instead. I mean, that's what we do, don't we?'

Carver didn't know what to reply. The lawyer Sally had fixed him up with in Lozier had told him that the law had nothing on him and that sooner or later they'd have to let him go. His plan had been to wait patiently for that to happen and then go back to Sally Bright, marry her and make a new life being on the right side of the law. Ketchum, by springing him from the cell in Lozier, had ruined all that. Now he wasn't sure if he could bear to see Sally again, knowing their future together could now no longer be.

'Well?' Ketchum asked him again, still playing his cruel game.

Looking at him, Carver felt a hatred for him welling up inside. He had shoved Deputy Board's gun into the waist of his trousers and he felt like drawing it now and shooting

Ketchum dead. He could go and get Sally and her children and the money and run away with her. They could start again somewhere way out West where no one would know who he was. But kill Ketchum? No one had achieved that yet and he didn't see that he'd be quick enough to be able to do so now. But if not now, maybe later.

'OK,' he said at last. 'Let's go back to Sal's and get the money.'

TWELVE

On hearing of what had happened in Lozier, Captain Foggerty felt vindicated for having held the belief that Lee Fox was not who he said he was and that he was in fact Will Carver, member of the notorious Ketchum gang. He became even more convinced that the money from the 14 May train robbery had been stashed somewhere on the Brights' homestead. He was within a day's riding of Tom Green County, where the Brights' homestead was, and decided to make a beeline for it. His belief was that this was where Ketchum and Carver would head.

Sally Bright was appalled when she heard what had happened to Deputy Board.

'Was he dead?' she asked Carver.

'I don't know but I guess so,' Carver replied.

113

They were talking in whispers to one another, not so much to avoid the ears of Ketchum but to avoid those of her children. The children had grown to love Will Carver but they were as ever wary of so gruff a character as Ketchum.

'What you gonna do?' Sally asked him.

'I don't know, Sal. My days of robbing and thieving are over but Tom's won't be until he's dead. Trouble is Texas Rangers are gonna know for sure now who I am. If we want to be together we're gonna have to clear right out of here, out of the State even, and start afresh somewhere else.'

'You think that can happen?' Sal asked anxiously.

'I think it's got to.'

Both of them knew it depended mainly on Ketchum.

'What about Tom?' Sal asked.

'You tell me,' was Carver's reply.

Ketchum had been attending to his ablutions at the washstand out in the open near the farmhouse. They'd arrived the evening before as it was getting dark. It'd been too late to bathe and he'd gone to bed unwashed. Now he was making a thorough job of it, even going so far as to trim his moustache in the most painstaking of ways. Sally and Carver watched him from a window in the farm-house.

'Why don't you just tell him to take all the money and go,' Sally suggested.

'Well, we won't get far without money, but it's not that, Sal. He plans to rob more trains and takes it for granted I'm gonna help him.'

'Well, can't you tell him you ain't?' Sally asked anxiously.

'You don't know Tom, if you think it's as simple as that. Dave and Sam are both dead. Tom ain't gonna be happy until he's paid the world back for that. He'll kill anyone now that tries to get between him and his intentions, me included.'

'What about the others?'

'The Wild Bunch, as the papers is calling them?' Carver queried. 'He's too wild for them. They like to think of themselves as gentlemen outlaws who are just in it for the money. Tom likes to think he walks in the shoes of the likes of Billy the Kid. It's not the money for him, it's the robbing and the killing. He can't get enough of it.'

'And what about you, Will?' Sally asked,

longing for the right answer.

'It was the money, until I met you.'

Ketchum had said about Carver that he was always falling in love and his words echoed in Sally's head now. She told Carver this. Turning towards her and taking her in his arms, he said, 'Of course there have been others, Sal, but none that I ever loved. I know that now. If I'd met you years ago I'd never have become an outlaw. And now that I've met you I don't want to be one any more. I want to live and look after you and the children. I feel now that that's what I was born to do. I felt it the first time I saw you but I know it all the more now.'

His words reassured Sally and she allowed herself to sink deeper into the strong arms of his embrace.

'I'll go with you anywhere,' she whispered. 'Even to the ends of the earth, so long as we can be together.'

This told Carver all he needed to know. Somehow or other he had to free himself of Ketchum. And soon, before the Texas Rangers showed up on their doorstep. He decided he had to go and talk to him.

'Tom,' he said approaching him at the

washstand where he was trimming the last few long hairs of his moustache. 'We need to talk.'

'Well, talk away,' was Ketchum's deceptively sanguine reply.

'We gotta get away from here before them Texas Rangers show up.'

'We'll leave today. We only came for the money. As soon as we've had breakfast we can go,' Ketchum replied.

It was obvious to Carver that he was purposely disregarding any concerns there might be about Sally and her family being seen to be accomplices of theirs and it made him angry.

'And what about Sally?' he asked. 'You don't think the Texas Rangers are gonna leave her be? They didn't before and they especially won't now.'

'Well,' Ketchum replied, turning away from the mirror he was watching his reflection in and looking pointedly into Carver's face. 'We can't take a woman with us, especially not one with children.'

'They'll search for the money, Tom.'

'But they won't find it.'

'And they'll burn the whole place down.'

117

Ketchum returned to looking in the mirror and trimming his moustache. He hadn't shrugged his shoulders but Carver felt he might just as well have, for all the signs he showed of caring about what happened to Sally and her children.

'We got trains to rob, Will. That's what we do. I keep saying it. Dave. Sam, you, me. It's what we all do and there ain't no getting away from it. 'Cause once we try to they're gonna not rest until they stretch our necks, family men or whatever else it is we decide to do instead.'

'I ain't leaving them, Tom. I can't and I won't.'

Ketchum made no immediate reply to what Carver said. His body tensed and Carver could see this. He waited for Ketchum's reply but it seemed an age in coming.

'Dave's dead,' he said, speaking at last, carrying on trimming the last few remaining long hairs of his moustache. 'She can have his share of the money and she can leave here. Go west to New Mexico or Arizona. Texas Rangers won't bother her none then.'

'And who's gonna protect her?'

'Can't see that that's any of our business,

118

but she'll have money enough to hire an army of men.'

Carver knew that Ketchum was purposely and callously disregarding how he knew he felt about Sally and it began to really get to him. He decided he had to face him head on over the matter.

'If anyone's gonna protect Sally, Tom, it's going to be me. I feel we got her into this trouble and now we gotta get her out of it. And besides I love her,' he said. 'I ain't going nowhere without her.'

Ketchum finished with trimming his moustache and put the scissors down. Taking one last look at himself in the mirror and satisfying himself that he looked as good as he could make himself look, he turned and began to walk in the direction of the farmhouse.

'Texas Rangers,' he said over his shoulder, 'might have different views on that.'

Captain Foggerty would indeed have had different views on the matter. He knew now beyond a shadow of a doubt who Lee Fox really was and that the man who had sprung him from the town jail was Tom Ketchum. Deputy Board had been lucky. The bullet wound he took from Ketchum's gun had just missed his heart and given him only a nasty shoulder wound. He had been able, therefore, to recount the Christian names the two outlaws had used in addressing one another to Sheriff Broom. The modern telegraph system was a marvel for keeping people at distances informed of the latest news and once Sheriff Broom knew the truth of Will Carver's identity he made sure Captain Foggerty was informed of it. Riders criss-crossed lower West Texas until Foggerty and his men were found. Once Foggerty had received the information he made a beeline for the one place he knew Ketchum must be heading for.

It was early afternoon, two days after the day Carver had spoken to Ketchum about his concerns over Sally Bright, when Foggerty and his men rode to the spot from which they had been able to survey the Brights' place all those months before.

'Looks fairly quiet down there, don't you think?' Foggerty remarked to his lieutenant, Barrett, as he peered through his binoculars.

'Sure does,' Barrett replied. 'But they could all be inside resting. It's pretty hot today.'

'Hmm,' Foggerty remarked, unconvinced. He was a man of experience and to him the place had the feel of being deserted. 'We'll just sit here for a while and see if there are any signs of movement. If not we'll go down and take a look.'

Foggerty was not a man of great patience where outlaws were concerned and after about twenty minutes of restless observation he led his men in a trot on to the Brights' place. It was no surprise to him to find there was no one there.

'Shall we search the place?' Barrett asked him.

'I shouldn't bother. They'll have taken the money with them,' was Foggerty's reply.

'So what now, sir?'

'Tracks. Let's try and find out which direction they went in. They won't be travelling very fast with a woman and three children in tow.'

'What makes you think they took 'em?' Barrett asked him.

'Well, they ain't here, are they?'

Barrett, feeling a little stupid, had to agree that this was the case.

It was soon established that one horse and

a wagon with a horse tied to the back of it had left the Brights' place heading due north-west.

'We'll catch 'em,' Foggerty declared.

'While we're here shall we take advantage of Mrs Bright's kitchen and have ourselves some food, sir?' Barrett asked. They hadn't eaten since dawn.

Foggerty took out a pocket-watch, looked at it and then looked up at the sky.

'No,' he replied. 'We got a couple of hours' riding-time yet. Best we take advantage of them.'

It wouldn't matter how much riding-time Captain Foggerty and his men gave themselves, they were not going to be able to catch up with their quarry. In the end Carver had settled for a compromise and he and Ketchum had taken Sally and the children to a hideout near Independence Creek at the top of Terrell County. It was difficult going and the wagon had not liked it but in the end they had made it, half a day ahead of where Foggerty found the ground was too hard for any tracks to be left. The hideout was not known to anyone, save the likes of Ketchum and his outlaw fraternity, and, while not comfortable, Sally would at least be safe there. It was Ketchum's view that she and the children could be left to hang out there for ever if necessary, but it was not Carver's.

'Tom, I want to talk to you,' he told Ketchum in a fit of exasperation as they sat around the camp-fire on the first night.

Getting up, he showed Ketchum that he wanted for the talk to be in private and he led him away to where the river flowed. Ketchum followed reluctantly. He was comfortable where he was sitting and he felt he could guess what Carver wanted to talk to him about. It was a topic he found boring.

'What is it you want of me?' Carver asked him when he felt they were far enough away from the camp-fire not to be heard by either Sally or the children.

'No, Will, the question is what have you always wanted of me?' Ketchum replied with a degree of venom that put Carver instantly on his guard. Carver was glad that, unlike the time at the washstand a couple of days before, he was this time armed.

'You had a gang, Tom and I was part of it.

That was all. What are you trying to make more of it for?'

'We stick together. That's why we've always made it.'

Carver in fact found this hard to take from Ketchum, who'd always in the past shown himself to be headstrong, unstable and never happy unless he was calling the shots and making everyone obey them or else. Carver knew that Ketchum was hurting over the loss of his brother and Dave Atkins, two men whose blind loyalty he had always been able to count upon, and that he was looking to replace that lost blind loyalty with his own. Well, as far as he was concerned, he wasn't going to get it from him. He'd never given it before and, besides, there was now anyway someone far more worthy of it.

'Why not try and find the others and join up with them?' he asked.

By the others he meant people like Ben Kilpatrick, Kid Curry and even the Sundance Kid and Butch Cassidy, the group of men better known as the Wild Bunch. They were all successful outlaws who were fast becoming living legends in the West. But they were in fact men who had turned their backs on the unstable and self-destructive Tom Ketchum. So his reaction was to spit venom about them.

'That bunch!' he snapped derogatively. 'They're slicker than calf slobbers and they ain't what I been used to.'

'But times are changing, Tom,' Carver remarked.

'I'm sick of hearing that. If times are a-changing it's only because the likes of you and them are going soft and letting it happen.'

'It ain't that. It's the law. They got too strong and well organized for us and that is about the long and short of it.'

Ketchum wasn't a man with a head for philosophical argument and he decided he didn't want to hear any more of what Carver had to say. He'd been enjoying a mug of good coffee when Will took him away from the camp-fire. He'd finished it while they were speaking and was going back there to get another.

'There's a train I got a mind to rob in the next few days, Will. Lozier way. I'm counting on you to help me to do it.'

And without giving Carver a chance to answer him he strode off back to where Sally was contemplating settling the children down for the night.

THIRTEEN

Carver went with Ketchum for the sake of Sally and the children. But before they left he insisted that Sally be given a third share of the money and told her that if anything happened to him, meaning that if he was killed or ended up in prison, she was to take it and go West and make a new life for herself and the children.

'But I will be back,' he promised her. 'Whatever Ketchum thinks he's got planned for me, his so-called gang, he'll find out I'm nobody's lap dog. If I think it's a good idea, I'll do it. If I don't, I won't. But whatever happens, I'll be back.'

Then, as he rode alongside Ketchum through backwoods country to Lozier, he couldn't help but think of Deputy Board. He figured he had to be dead, shot in the heart like that at point-blank range. Board had become his friend and Ketchum had killed him in cold blood. Whatever happened, Will decided, Ketchum was going to pay for it.

In Lozier, Captain Foggerty was having similar thoughts about Ketchum.

'He's somewhere and I ain't gonna stop until I find him,' he told Sheriff Broom as they sat drinking coffee.

'He's probably nearer than you think,' Broom remarked. 'Never thought they was anywhere near town when he came and sprung Lee Fox. I mean Will Carver,' he corrected himself.

'Yeah, well, I told you there was something suspicious about Carver. I never believed for one minute that he was who said he was.'

'Well, I wouldn't have done, except that he seemed so thoroughly decent a sort. Why, everyone who came into regular contact with him just got fonder and fonder of him, especially my deputy.'

'Outlaws ain't usually lacking in charm. It's just that it's generally the sort that costs people their lives, as your deputy came close to finding out.'

'He fair charmed Sally Bright, that's for sure,' Broom agreed, 'though rumour always had it that her husband weren't as straight as he would have people believe.'

'Yeah, well, whatever. She's thrown in her lot with them and that makes her as bad as them.'

Broom felt like denying the fact but didn't think he should contradict the wisdom of a man whose life was dedicated to cleaning up Texas. Instead he asked, 'So what now, Captain?'

'We're pulling out tonight, heading for the canyons. I reckon that's where they're hanging out. There's a full moon and that'll give us enough light to ride by,' Foggerty replied.

Ketchum had been asked a similar question by Carver, as they sat drinking coffee beside a camp-fire a little distance outside Lozier.

'We're gonna take the express out of Lozier tonight,' he answered him.

Carver didn't say anything in reply but just nodded in acquiescence.

'Yeah, and I gotta plan,' Ketchum continued. 'There ain't enough of us to stage a hold-up, so I reckon if I boarded the train as it was taking on water at Lozier, you could be waiting down the line at Cuttings Bend. We could separate the express car from the carriages and blow open the safe further down the line. Should be a cinch.'

Reformed though he wanted to be, Carver couldn't help but be struck by the clever simplicity of the plan. It was going to be his last robbery, of this he was determined, but he didn't know how he was going to make it so. He was hoping that, by some fluke, Ketchum would get killed as he tried to carry it out, but equally he knew he couldn't count on it happening. Whether, though, he could shoot him down in cold blood when he least expected it, he wasn't sure. But had Ketchum given him another way out? Could he not simply make a dash for it when Ketchum left to go to Lozier to board the train? No, he thought, it would be too uncertain an escape from his clutches. Being Ketchum, he'd probably successfully complete the robbery and live to hunt him down. No, he thought, returning to the only conclusion possible, Ketchum had to die.

'Ok,' he said to him regarding his plan for robbing the train. 'Seems like a good idea to me. You got enough dynamite?'

About the time the train was gathering speed after pulling out of Lozier, Captain Foggerty ordered his men to mount their horses. Sheriff Broom was there to see them off.

'Which way you going?' he asked Foggerty.

'Thought we'd follow the railway line to Cuttings Bend and then cut across country,' Foggerty replied. 'Railway line shows up good in the moonlight.'

'Well, good luck,' Sheriff Broom said to him.

'Thank you. We'll be back,' was Foggerty's reply, as he kicked his horse into a trot and pointed it to follow the railway line out of town.

Ketchum had climbed onto the footplate of the locomotive as it pulled out of Lozier. Amid the noise of the train as it got up a head of steam to pull out of the station, he was able to remain undetected. Then, when the train had gone a mile down the track, he suddenly presented himself to the engineer, Joseph Kirchgrabber and the fireman, John Scanlon.

Waving a Winchester at them, he took over the train, ordering Kirchgrabber to stop as they entered the curve of Cuttings Bend. There waiting with the horses was Will Carver.

Carver knew what he had to and quickly climbed into the baggage car, ordering the messenger, Charles Drew to put his hands up.

'We gotta uncouple the train,' Ketchum called out to Carver, while keeping his rifle trained on the engineer. 'Get down there and do it,' he ordered the fireman. He wanted to get the locomotive and the baggage car away before the passengers and the guard knew what had happened. He and Carver were too few to put up a fight if trouble started.

'You won't get this train uncoupled on a bend,' the fireman told him. 'Ain't you heard of the "Miller Hook"? This train's got 'em and they don't allow for no uncoupling on a bend.'

'Don't give me no shit,' Ketchum snarled at him. 'Just do as I tell you.'

Scanlon was the kind of man who liked to have the last laugh and so simply set about trying to do what he'd been ordered to do. Making a great show of it, he tried to undo the couplings, knowing they would not shift.

'Come on!' Ketchum snarled at him impatiently.

Scanlon continued to struggle with the couplings but, of course, to no avail. As the tension began to build and Ketchum began to want to shoot the man for failing so miserably to do what he'd been ordered to do a shot rang out, just missing his head. It was the mail clerk, poking his head out of the express car and taking a pot shot at what he guessed to be an outlaw. The shot, having missed Ketchum, ricocheted off the steel wall of the fireman's place and smacked the engineer in the face, breaking his jaw. As Ketchum went to fire back in the direction of the mail clerk, Scanlon suddenly called out that he had done it.

'Right,' snapped Ketchum. 'Get up here and drive this train.'

What Scanlon had in fact done was undo the airhose serving the brakes causing the brakes on all the carriage wheels to lock.

'All right, all right,' he sang out, climbing aboard the footplate of the locomotive.

He pushed the controls of the train to try and make it go forward but the wheels of the locomotive simply spun on the tracks, causing them to grind and throw up sparks.

'What the hell's happening? Ketchum snarled at him. 'Get this train moving.'

'I told you,' Scanlon reminded him, 'you can't uncouple this train on a bend. Now the brakes have seized.'

Scanlon was indeed having the last laugh but it really would be the last laugh he would ever have. For Ketchum, realizing that everything was going badly wrong, emptied his Winchester into his back and he fell into a heap, dying.

'Damn you!' Ketchum snarled at him, before jumping off the train.

As he did so the mail clerk poked his head out of the express car again, ready to take what would have been an easy shot at him. But Ketchum, as always, was not off his guard. Before the mail clerk could pull the trigger of his carbine Ketchum blasted him to kingdom come. Then he hurried on to the baggage car.

'Get the dynamite, Will,' he called out to Carver, 'we're gonna have to blow the safe here.'

Enough shots had rung out in what was the

still of the night to fill the air for miles around and Captain Foggerty and his men heard them. Captain Foggerty, pulling up his horse, turned to Lieutenant Barrett and said, 'You hear what I hear?'

'I sure do,' Barrett replied. Both men knew the shots had come from somewhere in front of them down the line. 'Someone must be holding up the train.'

'You ain't kidding,' was Foggerty's reply, as he kicked his horse and led his men in a gallop down the line. It wasn't long before the lights of the train became visible.

The first person to hear what he took to be a troop of men coming at speed towards them was Carver. He was standing by the horses taking dynamite out of his saddle-bags.

My God, he thought. Could they be Texas Rangers?

Whoever they were, he did not want to confront them. This, he knew, had to be the opportunity he was waiting for. He doubted if Ketchum, who was still in the baggage car of the train, had heard the troop of men coming and even if he had it would be too late now. He'd never be able to make good a quick get-away, whereas he himself could. Without wasting a second more thinking about it, he swung up onto his horse and spurred it into a gallop north-west away from the scene. Neither Foggerty, nor any of his men, saw him do it. It wasn't long before they drew up level with the baggage car.

What the. . . ? Ketchum asked himself in startled tones as through the wide carriage car-doors he saw the Texas Rangers arrive.

Without pausing for a second, he opened fire on the troop of men. As one of their company fell Foggerty quickly ordered the rest to get out of the way. But there was no need. Unnoticed by Ketchum, Charles Drew had made a grab for his shotgun. As Ketchum unloaded his Winchester in the direction of the Texas Rangers, Drew opened fire, almost at point blank range, sending a load of lead tearing into his arm at the elbow. It spun Ketchum around and threw him crashing into a wall of the carriage. He had hardly come to lie still when Drew was standing above him with his fingers on the trigger of the second barrel, ready to fill him with its contents.

'Well, done, sir!' Foggerty congratulated the messenger. 'Is he the only one?'

'There was another but he must have seen you coming and fled. He went to get some dynamite.'

'Anyone hurt?' Foggerty asked, 'apart from this low-life piece of shit?'

Drew had to report that he didn't know but Foggerty was soon to discover the extent of Ketchum's murderous attempt to rob the train.

'This is hanging stuff,' he said to Ketchum, with the lawman's satisfied glint in his eye, as he was pulled from the baggage car. 'Now are you gonna tell me who was with you or am I gonna have to beat it out of you?'

Ketchum was in too much agony from the wound to his arm, which had been practically severed, to make any kind of reply. But this did not bother Foggerty. He felt he knew what the answer was but he wanted to hear it from Ketchum's lips. But Ketchum was tougher than that and kept tight-lipped. Foggerty questioned him but then began to fear that he might die from loss of blood and rob them all of the satisfaction of seeing him hang.

'All right,' he said to Barrett, 'put a tourniquet on that arm and let's get him back to

Lozier. The doctor can patch him up and then we can question him again.'

As Barrett did as he was instructed, Foggerty stood back and looked around him. It had to be Will Carver who had been Ketchum's accomplice, of this he was sure. He would not have let Sally Bright and the children travel far alone, which meant, he concluded, they must be hiding somewhere not too far away. But where? He asked himself, again looking all around him into the darkness that surrounded them. Where?

FOURTEEN

Carver rode without stopping all night. He was fairly certain he wasn't being followed, but he couldn't be sure. There was a full moon and anyone who was determined to give chase could do so without too much difficulty. Dawn arrived about the time he reached the mouth of the canyons. By this time, it was more than apparent to him that he had in fact not been followed. Still, he made thoroughly sure before making his horse follow the track that would take him to where Sally and the children were hiding out.

Sally, always a light sleeper, heard him coming. She'd been left with a Winchester rifle and had grabbed it and placed herself behind a rock with the trigger cocked just in case he was someone else. Relieved when she saw that it was indeed him, she showed herself and hurried to greet him.

'Will,' she said. 'Back so soon?'

'Yes,' he said, jumping down from his horse and taking her in his arms, something they had not been free to do since the time he was arrested by Foggerty and locked up in Lozier.

'No Tom?' Sally asked him.

'Texas Rangers or someone came upon us while we was holding up the train. I was able to escape but Tom wasn't. He's either dead or been taken prisoner.'

'You don't know which?' Sally asked, relieved that he wasn't there to rule their lives any more and keen to know if it would be for good.

'I told you,' Carver replied, 'I didn't hang around, so I don't know.'

'What now?' Sally asked, still embracing Carver.

'That's what we gotta think about,' he replied, giving her one more hug and then breaking free. 'Meanwhile I need some coffee.'

'Yes, of course, dear,' Sally said, going to the camp-fire and poking at the ashes to rekindle it.

*

In Lozier Ketchum was languishing in the cell from which he had sprung Carver less than a week before. He'd been brought in the middle of the night but already, barely an hour after sun-up, the whole town knew he was there. By mid-morning they were clamouring for a lynching.

'You're lucky you got the Texas Rangers here to protect you,' Sheriff Broom informed him. 'I don't think I could hold the town by myself.'

Ketchum hardly cared though, at least not at that moment. Lozier didn't have its own doctor and there was not one visiting the town at the time. His arm was a bloody mess and it looked bad.

'When you gonna get me a doctor?' was all Ketchum said in reply.

'I told you we ain't got one in town yet, but we sent for the one in Langtry to come and see you. He'll be here, I guess, as soon as he can be.'

Broom could remember his deputy lying in pain and at death's door after Ketchum had shot him and he didn't feel a lot of sympathy

141

for Ketchum now in his own hour of need.

'I'll be dead before he gets here,' Ketchum groaned, more to himself than out loud.

That you could be, Sheriff Broom couldn't but help think to himself, but not from your arm wound.

Just at that point Captain Foggerty appeared at the door of his office and came in. He and Broom greeted one another and then Foggerty said, 'Seems like there's lynching fever beginning to grip this town, Jed. Your people easily pacified?'

'Yeah, well, I was just saying to Ketchum here that I didn't reckon his chances much if you hadn't been here to protect him.'

'And I said "where's the doctor?"' Ketchum interrupted them.

He was beginning to sound and look feverish and Foggerty began to fear that Texas State Law might be in danger of losing an opportunity to demonstrate to its citizens what happened to people who flew in the face of it. And, what was more, he didn't want to lose the chance of interrogating him.

'And I told you he'd be here just as quickly as he could be,' Sheriff Broom remarked.

Foggerty looked at him questioningly and

Broom felt he could guess what he was thinking.

'Which should be any time now,' he added to what he had already said.

'Good,' Foggerty remarked, before asking, 'You got some coffee on the go?'

Carver was nervous about leaving the camp. He didn't know if the Texas Rangers would be scouring the countryside looking for him. In fact Foggerty had sent some of his men out to scout around, but looking for Carver in the canyons would be like looking for a needle in a haystack. In some way Carver thought he should just give himself up and throw himself on the mercy of the courts, but equally he knew that would be a risky business. He could get the rope – he had killed men – or he could get the long stretch inside, either of which would separate him from Sally, which he didn't want. The West was still big enough for a man to lose himself in and he decided that this was what he had to do.

Good guy or bad guy, Carver felt all he'd done he'd done to survive. It was all he was doing now. There were bad guys turning law enforcers and they were being accepted into the good citizenry of the United States of America.

He had it in mind to become a farmer. Shouldn't that be just as acceptable? And he had the money to do it; all he and Sally had to do was get out of Texas and he could really make it. Become a good citizen. Maybe, who knows, in some new community evolving into a town he could lend his skills to becoming a law enforcer.

These were not the thoughts Tom Ketchum was having. The doctor had arrived and declared that his arm was going to have to be amputated. It was his shooting arm and without it he suddenly felt quite helpless. He spent days practising drawing with his left hand, but without a gun to weight it with he felt it was a useless exercise. Then he was tried and found guilty of murder and sentenced to hang. Hanging was the thing he had dreaded most throughout his entire career as an outlaw. As a child he had nearly drowned once and it had left him with a phobia about anything to do with his airways being restricted. Standing in the dock when the sentence was pronounced he decided there and then that there was no way any hangman was going to get the chance to put a noose around his neck.

He was wrong, though, for despite one escape attempt, two suicide attempts and two appeals, he was eventually lead to the scaffold. It was his bad luck, though, that the man appointed to hang him was not an experienced hangman. His name was Salome Garcia and he was Terrel County Sheriff.

'I ain't exactly sure how long the drop should be,' he remarked to one of his colleagues.

'Well, ain't there a table that tells you?' the colleague, a governor's appointee named Lewis C. Fort asked him.

'Not one that I've ever had sight of. In the past I've sort of used my instincts.'

'And things usually turned out satisfactory enough?'

'Well, they have,' replied Garcia, 'but you gotta be careful you don't go ripping off the head of the man you're hanging. I've heard of that happening before now.'

'Can't say it would worry me one way or the other how Ketchum dies, as long as he does,' Fort declared emphatically.

'Maybe, but I'm a man as likes to get things

right,' Garcia said just as emphatically.

On the basis of Ketchum's weight, which was 193 pounds, it was decided in the end that the rope should be five feet nine inches long. Any experienced hangman could have told them that this was too long. So that was bad enough. But even worse was that in the measuring out of it someone got their sums wrong and the noose that was placed around Ketchum's neck on the appointed day of execution 26 April 1901, was a good eighteen inches longer.

Luckily, if any degree of mercy is to be granted a murderous, probably psychotic, outlaw, Ketchum was not aware of any of the problems that existed in trying to decide how most efficiently to hang him. But, nevertheless, he was in a panic the morning they came to lead him to the gallows. He'd been offered a good breakfast but had not been able to swallow a morsel of it. Instead, he had built and smoked nigh on fifty cigarettes.

He was in a panic but he wasn't going to let the bastards see it. He might even try and escape. One of the guards sent to accompany him to the gallows seemed to hold his rifle very casually. Problem was he only had one arm and to handle a rifle reliably he knew you needed two.

Then they strapped his hands behind his back. His only other thought then was to launch himself to fly head first over the scaffolding railings. But as he mounted the scaffolding steps he saw that this was going to be impossible, being, as it seemed, half the world had turned out to assist the hangman.

It wasn't long before the noose was put around his neck. There were already beads of sweat on his forehead and now his Adam's apple bulged in his neck. He badly needed a smoke. Just one more drag on a cigarette to calm his nerves. Other than to read out a notice, no one had spoken directly to him. He would have asked for a cigarette now, but his throat and tongue were dry and he wouldn't have been able to form the words.

Next a black hood was put over his head and he heard the steps of the people that had surrounded him moving away. It was going to happen, he thought, any minute now. His mind turned to the rope sitting like a necklace on his neck. It seemed too thin. He was no expert on the matter, but he felt it should have been thicker. And it seemed wet or greasy. Then he felt someone take a heavy footstep on the floorboards near him and next he was falling, falling, falling until he had no living faculties left to be aware of anything.

'My God!' someone on the ground was heard to exclaim.

Other people simply gasped, while County Sheriff Garcia gulped with embarrassment. He had got it wrong and they had indeed decapitated Ketchum.

FIFTEEN

Carver knew nothing about Ketchum's grisly death until he read about it in a newspaper some time later. He was in a general store in a small town called Buckeye near where he was establishing himself as a farmer in Arizona. No one knew about his past and he was confident that this was the way it would remain.

'Got a paper?' he asked the store's proprietor.

'Sure thing, Rod,' the store owner replied.

Carver took it and put it with his supplies. Then with the help of the store's boy he loaded his purchases onto the back of a buckwagon.

He had a few other things to do in town,

like getting a haircut and enjoying a beer in his favoured saloon. It wasn't until he was back at home a few hours later that he found the time to read the paper. Then on the inside page he came across the story of how the hanging of notorious outlaw Thomas Ketchum had been bungled so badly. Carver read the whole story through and then again in appalled silence. Sally was busy about the house and he didn't call her immediately. He had to have time to take it all in. He hadn't exactly liked Ketchum but then again he hadn't hated him either. They'd been through a lot together and a bond of sorts – that which exists between thieves – had grown up between them and he would not have wished so horrible a death upon him. At last he called Sally over to take a look at the story.

'My God, poor Tom!' she exclaimed out loud, feeling her stomach turn and putting a hand to her mouth.

'Yeah, what a way to die,' Carver agreed with her. 'I wouldn't have wished that upon my worst enemy.'

Also mentioned in the story was Carver's name. The reporter said that he was the only surviving member of Ketchum's gang and that he was still on the run. The sight of his name in print, a name that he hadn't known himself by for nigh on two years now, made the hairs on the back of his head stand on end. Neither he nor Sally said it, but they both knew he could just as easily have been hanged along side Ketchum, maybe even have shared the same fate as him.

'At least,' Sally remarked, handing him back the paper and going and sitting down in a chair opposite him, 'they didn't print your photograph.'

'Yeah,' he agreed, 'even with this beard someone might have recognized me. Best we don't leave the paper around for the children to see.'

'No, it's sure to upset them. Tom weren't no bad man to them. He was just Uncle Tom.'

'No,' Carver remarked abstractedly, his thoughts dwelling on something said in the report right at its very end. Sally hadn't read the whole of the story and for this he was glad, for what his mind was dwelling upon now was a comment reportedly made by Captain Foggerty.

I'm retiring soon but I would like the likes of William Carver to know that I ain't retiring entirely.

This was all that was quoted.

Another year went by and Carver began seriously to prosper as a farmer. People said it was because he didn't have to borrow money, that he hadn't had to put his farm in hock to the bank like the rest of them had. Well, that was true, he hadn't. Another man who was doing well in his newly chosen profession was Captain Foggerty. On retiring from the Texas Rangers he turned bounty hunter and a very successful one at that. People said he always got his man. Well, so he did. Top of his list now was Will Carver. Carver happened to be in Buckeye one warm September day when Foggerty rode into town. He recognized Foggerty long before Foggerty recognized him. But he was not the kind of man who went into a panic and he decided to go about his business as normal and to wait and see what happened.

Foggerty's first port of call was the sheriff's office. Buckeye was a peaceable sort of town and the sheriff was a bluff sort of character whose life was rarely bothered by anything that could seriously be described as crime.

'No,' he replied to Foggerty's question as to whether or not he had seen anyone with a likeness to the picture of the wanted notice for Will Carver that he showed him. 'Can't say I have.'

'He's been known to go by various names. Lee Fox, for instance.'

'No,' replied sheriff, whose name was Don Patten, 'ain't ever heard of anyone around these parts going by any such name.'

Foggerty wasn't surprised by Patten's answers. It was the usual kind of offhand response he got from people in the quiet backwaters of the West.

'Well, then,' he persevered, 'can you give me a list of the names of all the newcomers to the county in, say, the last two years.'

'Well, it ain't exactly my job to know them. You'd do better to go to the mayor's office to look for that kind of information,' Sheriff Patten replied in a relaxed kind of drawl.

His tone and manner began to annoy

Foggerty and he decided he was wasting his time.

'Well,' he said to Patten, getting ready to leave his office, 'Buckeye ain't exactly hell on earth, which is what the likes of Will Carver can easily turn it into. I suppose if he'd have been here, you'd have known it.'

'Sorry I ain't been able to help much,' Patten said.

'Well, I'll be in town a few days, if you can think of anything, just let me know.'

'Sure thing,' Patten replied.

Carver, who was loading provisions onto his buckboard, saw Foggerty step out of Sheriff Patten's office. His beard was bushy and covered most of his face and he reckoned that with it Foggerty was unlikely to recognize him from a distance. But he wasn't going to take any chances and he decided to hurry up loading his provisions and to get out of town. Sheriff Patten wouldn't have known anything and he didn't reckon there was anything he could have said to Foggerty that would have made him think he was present in the county.

The problem was, though, Foggerty had stepped off the plankwalk and was heading his way. Keeping his head down, Carver went back into the store to collect the last of his purchases. The store wasn't busy and the storekeeper, as he often did, would have liked to keep Carver talking, but Carver made it look as if he was suddenly in a hurry.

'Well, anyway, say hello to Sally and the girls for me,' the storekeeper said to Carver as he was leaving.

He was a big man with a booming voice that carried. Foggerty had only got as far as the plank-walk and was about to step on to it when the storekeeper had called out to Carver to be remembered to Sally, who was now in fact Mrs Rod Pearson. But he was close enough to hear 'Sally'. There was only one Sally that had ever figured, and continued to figure, in his thoughts. If she was anywhere, she was likely to be with the man he was hunting. Cool as he always was, Foggerty showed no signs of being affected by what he had just heard. Carver, though, knew he must have been.

His and Foggerty's paths crossed on the plankwalk, as he came out of the store and Foggerty went to go in.

'Afternoon,' Foggerty said in a civilized sort of manner as he passed him.

As he spoke he knew that here was his man. There was fear in his eyes, as there had been in Sally Bright's barn, and it gave them a look he easily recognized.

'Afternoon,' Carver replied, beads of sweat already forming on his brow.

Foggerty noticed that Carver was not wearing a gun. It was the perfect opportunity. But by the time he had stopped and turned around Carver had reached his buckboard, where he always kept a carbine hidden.

'Will Carver,' Foggerty called out, drawing a sixgun.

As he spoke the words, the fingers of Carver's right hand closed on the carbine and in a flash he pulled it from where it was concealed and had it aimed at Foggerty. He did not want to kill him but the beating he'd taken at his hands and the harsh way he had dealt with Sally flashed through his mind as he stood with his finger wrapped around the trigger of the carbine poised to protect his life.

'I ain't Will Carver,' he said clearly and loudly. 'You've got the wrong man, mister.'

'Drop it, Carver,' were all the words Foggerty said.

But it was obvious to him Carver was going to do no such thing. He was wanted dead or alive. It made no diffeience to him how he took him. Aiming to shoot him between the eyes he pulled the trigger of his gun. Nothing happened. The damn thing had jammed. He tried to fire it again but still nothing happened. Thinking quickly, Carver knew he had to fire his own weapon. It would be in self-defence and Foggerty would be gone for ever. He only fired one shot and it took a beleaguered Foggerty to the promised land.

It wasn't long before Sheriff Patten, who'd heard the shot, came running from his office to see what had happened.

'He seemed to think I was someone else,' Carver informed him.

'Yeah,' agreed the storekeeper. 'I saw it and then he drew on him. Rod had no choice. It was self-defence. Pure and simple.'

'Bounty hunters,' remarked Sheriff Patten. 'I ain't ever had no time for them. I told him there was no one around here called Will Carver, nor anyone that looked like the face on the Wanted poster he showed me. But he didn't seem to want to believe me.'

'Yeah, well,' was all Carver said in reply. 'Best I get on home now to Sally and the girls.'

As he climbed on the buckboard and rode the journey home Carver had a lot to think over, not least of all being, was it safe to stay put or did he have to think now of moving on?